The Coconut Seller 里

Jack Scholes 著

李璞良 譯

U0025455

ABOUT THIS BOOK

For the Student 🎧 Listen to the story and do some activities on your Audio CD.
💬 Talk about the story.

For the teacher Go to our Readers Resource site for information on using readers and downloadable Resource Sheets, photocopiable Worksheets, and Tapescripts. www.helblingreaders.com

You can download the Answer Key from the official site of Cosmos Publisher: www.icosmos.com.tw

For lots of great ideas on using Graded Readers consult Reading Matters, the Teacher's Guide to using Helbling Readers.

Structures

Modal verb would	Non-defining relative clauses
I'd love to . . .	Present perfect continuous
Future continuous	Used to / would
Present perfect future	Used to / used to doing
Reported speech / verbs / questions	Second conditional
Past perfect	Expressing wishes and regrets
Defining relative clauses	

Structures from lower levels are also included.

CONTENTS

MEET THE AUTHOR

Dear Jack, tell us a little about yourself.

I was born in the North of England and studied German[1] and Russian[2] at Liverpool University. After graduation I spent several years traveling around the world, teaching English to finance[3] the trips.

I then went back to England to do a postgraduate[4] course at London University. I came to Brazil in 1976 and have lived and worked here, teaching and writing, ever since.

When did you start writing stories?

My first story was published in 1999. This is now my tenth book.

How do you think of your stories?

Stories are around us all the time, often begging to be written, but we rarely take much notice of them. Stories seem to find me, rather than me consciously[5] looking for one. My inspiration[6] often comes from a real event.

What is the message in this story?

There are several messages in the story, but I think the most powerful one can be summed up[7] in the words of the English teacher in the film *Dead Poets Society*—"Seize[8] the day! Make your lives extraordinary[9]!" We *can* change things. We *can* live the life we want and realize our full potential[10].

Have you any other stories planned for the future?

Yes, I have a file full of ideas for stories.

1 German [ˋdʒɝmən] (n.) 德語
2 Russian [ˋrʌʃən] (n.) 俄語
3 finance [faɪˋnæns] (v.) 籌措資金
4 postgraduate [postˋgrædʒuɪt] (a.) 研究生的
5 consciously [ˋkɑnʃənslɪ] (adv.) 有意識地
6 inspiration [ˏɪnspəˋreʃən] (n.) 靈感
7 sum up 總結
8 seize [siz] (v.) 抓住
9 extraordinary [ɪkˋstrɔrdnˏɛrɪ] (a.) 非凡的
10 potential [pəˋtɛnʃəl] (n.) 可能性；潛力

Map of Brazil

Cristo Redentor

1 The story *The Coconut Seller* takes place in Brazil. How much do you know about Brazil? Do the quiz and find out.

[a] Which city is the capital of Brazil?
   ① Rio de Janeiro.   ② Brasília.   ③ São Paulo.

[b] What is the estimated population of Brazil?
   ① About 50 million.
   ② Just over 100 million.
   ③ Nearly 200 million.

[c] Which is the largest city in Brazil?
   ① São Paulo.   ② Salvador.   ③ Rio de Janeiro.

[d] What is the official language in Brazil?
   ① Spanish.   ② French.   ③ Portuguese.

e ⃞ Which country was Brazil a colony of?

   ⃞ Portugal.   ⃞ Great Britain.   ⃞ Spain.

f ⃞ What is the name of the currency in Brazil?

   ⃞ Dollar.   ⃞ Real.   ⃞ Peso.

g ⃞ Brazil's large territory includes different ecosystems, such as

   ⃞ the Amazon Rainforest.
   ⃞ the Great Barrier Reef.
   ⃞ the Atacama Desert.

h ⃞ What is the famous Sugarloaf in Brazil?

   ⃞ A typical sweet.
   ⃞ A mountain in Rio de Janeiro.
   c ⃞ A popular beach in Bahia.

i ⃞ Which of the following is NOT a famous beach in Rio de Janeiro?

   ⃞ Copacabana.   ⃞ Ipanema.   ⃞ Pantanal.

j ⃞ What is samba?

   ⃞ A type of Brazilian dance and music genre.
   ⃞ A typical Brazilian dish.
   ⃞ A Brazilian festival.

2 Listen and check the answers.

3 With a partner write a quiz about another country you know or would like to visit. Then exchange your quiz with another pair.

4 Check you know the meanings of the words below. They are all used in the story to describe three of the main characters: Bruno, Clara and Zeca. Put the words you think might refer to each of them in the column below each picture.

poor	tough	bad-tempered	optimistic	rich
menacing	enthusiastic	muscular	gorgeous	thug
hard-working	fair-skinned	anxious	criminal	shy

Bruno	Clara	Zeca
....	....	....
....	....	....
....	....	....
....	....	....
....		

5 One of the three people above is the coconut seller. Who do you think it is? Who do you think are the hero and the villain in this story? Give reasons.

6 Look quickly at the cover of the book and the pictures inside. Then answer the questions.

a What kind of story is it? Tick.
- ☐ thriller / horror
- ☐ science fiction
- ☐ adventure / drama
- ☐ romantic comedy

b What do you think happens in the story? Tick two items.
- ☐ a robbery
- ☐ a fatal accident
- ☐ somebody is kidnapped
- ☐ dreams comes true

7 In pairs choose a picture from the book and write a description. Then describe the picture to another pair. See if they can guess which picture it is.

8 Match the informal words and expressions from the book to their meanings.

____ a rack one's brains	1 be cheerful and think of the positive aspects
____ b look on the bright side	2 busy movement of a lot of people
____ c hustle and bustle	3 go off in a noisy and angry way
____ d picture in your mind's eye	4 I agree
____ e seize the day	5 leave me alone
____ f go figure	6 not what I like
____ g give me a break	7 see in your imagination
____ h storm off	8 take an opportunity as soon as it appears
____ i it's a deal	9 tell you about
____ j set in his ways	10 think a lot
____ k not my scene	11 try to understand
____ l fill you in on	12 who always does the same things

9 How far do you agree with the following statements? Circle a score from 1 to 5 (1 = I totally disagree; 5 = I totally agree) for each one. Give your reasons and discuss with other students.

a) We can change our lives. We can live the life we want. ① ② ③ ④ ⑤

b) A movie or a book can really impress you and completely change your way of thinking. ① ② ③ ④ ⑤

c) It is important to be polite to other people. ① ② ③ ④ ⑤

d) It is better to be rich and unhappy than poor and happy. ① ② ③ ④ ⑤

e) Parents should know everything about your lives. ① ② ③ ④ ⑤

f) Sometimes you have to pretend to be something or someone you are not. You can't always be yourself. ① ② ③ ④ ⑤

g) You should only go out with people of the same race or from the same background as yourself. ① ② ③ ④ ⑤

h) Parents' opinions about the person you are going out with are very important. ① ② ③ ④ ⑤

i) It's okay to bully people who are smaller or weaker than yourself. ① ② ③ ④ ⑤

j) "The end justifies the means." This saying means that bad or unfair methods are acceptable if they allow you to achieve what you want, especially something good. ① ② ③ ④ ⑤

10 Listen to these four extracts from the book and match each one to the chapter it was taken from.

☐ Bruno

☐ Bruno meets Clara

☐ Bruno meets Clara's father   ☐ The abandoned factory

11 Choose one of the pictures above and imagine you are in the scene. Describe it in detail.

BRUNO

Bruno stopped what he was doing for a moment and sat down on a low wall in front of the beach. He stared out to sea with a broad[1] smile on his face, lost in thought as he enjoyed a moment's rest.

It was a hot, sultry[2] day like most summer days in Rio de Janeiro. It was only 11 o'clock in the morning and the temperature was already 35ºC, and the humidity[3] 82%. As usual, Bruno was wearing colorful, knee-length Bermuda[4] shorts, a white sleeveless T-shirt, and a pair of blue flip-flops[5]. The warm sea breeze[6] felt good against the smooth, dark skin of his face.

This was the day Bruno's life was going to change forever.

A group of girls walked past and smiled over at Bruno. He was slim and good-looking with short jet-black[7] hair and sparkling[8] dark brown eyes. But Bruno wasn't just another good-looking guy. He was one of life's genuine nice guys. He had a very distinctive[9], deep voice that was also pleasant and cheerful and warm. But he didn't use his voice to win people over[10]. No, whenever Bruno did say anything, it was always relevant[11] and meaningful.

---

1 broad [brɔd] (a.) 寬闊的
2 sultry [ˋsʌltrɪ] (a.) 悶熱的
3 humidity [hjuˋmɪdətɪ] (n.) 濕度
4 Bermuda [bɚˋmjudə] (n.) 百慕達
5 flip-flops [ˋflɪpˏflɑps] (n.) 〔複〕夾腳拖鞋
6 breeze [briz] (n.) 微風

7 jet-black [ˋdʒɛtˏblæk] (a.) 烏黑的
8 sparkling [ˋspɑrklɪŋ] (a.) 閃爍的
9 distinctive [dɪˋstɪŋktɪv] (a.) 有特色的
10 win over 說服
11 relevant [ˋrɛləvənt] (a.) 切題的

His classmates at school teased[1] him about being shy, but Bruno never got embarrassed or nervous; it was just the way he was. He kept himself to himself. And only spoke when he had something to say. Oh, and he had one of those irresistible[2] smiles that light up your day. And he constantly[3] looked on the bright side of things and was optimistic[4] about everything. Quite simply, he was a nice happy guy and you couldn't help but like him.

Bruno gazed[5] blankly at the hustle[6] and bustle[7] on Ipanema beach. The beach was crowded with rich, beautiful people, mainly Brazilians[8], but there were also lots of wealthy tourists, too. There were the usual sunworshippers[9] and surfers[10], and several groups of people playing football, volleyball and footvolley[11], a combination of volleyball and football which was invented in Brazil.

Bruno looked to his right at the two mountains in the distance—the "Dois Irmãos"—the Two Brothers. Rio is such a beautiful place to live, he thought to himself.

BRAZIL

- What do you know about Brazil? Think; then share ideas with a partner.
- What is your country famous for? What tourist attractions are there?

1 tease [tiz] (v.) 取笑
2 irresistible [ˌɪrɪˈzɪstəb!] (a.) 難以抗拒的
3 constantly [ˈkɑnstəntlɪ] (adv.) 不斷地
4 optimistic [ˌɑptəˈmɪstɪk] (a.) 樂觀的
5 gaze [gez] (v.) 凝視;注視
6 hustle [ˈhʌs!] (n.) 忙碌
7 bustle [ˈbʌs!] (n.) 喧嚣

8 Brazilian [brəˈzɪljən] (n.) 巴西人
9 sunworshipper [ˈsʌnˌwɜʃəpɚ] 〔口〕喜歡曬太陽的人
10 surfer [ˈsɝfɚ] (n.) 衝浪者
11 footvolley [ˈfʊtˌvɑlɪ] (n.) 足排球
12 sophisticated [səˈfɪstɪˌketɪd] (a.) 精緻的
13 favela [fəˈvɛlə] (n.) （巴西的）貧民區

Then he turned
around and looked at all the
sophisticated[12], high-rise apartment buildings along
the beach front. Ipanema was one of the best and most
expensive places to live in Rio. But Bruno was really thinking
of where *he* lived. Bruno lived in a favela[13], a kind of poor
shanty[14] town, called Morro do Cantagalo, on the hill, behind
these expensive flats.

In his mind's eye[15] he pictured the favela: hundreds of
small, shabby[16], randomly[17] built huts[18] all crowded close
together on the hillside. He thought about the thousands
of poor people living there, moving up and down along
the complex[19] network of stairways and tracks[20], often on
steep[21] inclines[22]. The narrow winding alleys[23] were too small
and dangerous for cars and other vehicles.

14 shanty [ˈʃæntɪ] (n.) 簡陋小屋
15 mind's eye 內心裡想像的畫面
16 shabby [ˈʃæbɪ] (a.) 破爛的
17 randomly [ˈrændəmlɪ] (adv.) 任意地
18 hut [hʌt] (n.) 簡陋的小屋

19 complex [ˈkɑmplɛks] (a.) 複雜的
20 track [træk] (n.) 小徑
21 steep [stip] (a.) 陡峭的
22 incline [ɪnˈklaɪn] (n.) 斜坡
23 alley [ˈælɪ] (n.) 巷子；胡同

The favela certainly wasn't an easy place to live and young people often turned to a life of crime[1]. Bruno suddenly thought of Zeca. Zeca started stealing when he was only eight years old, now he was the neighborhood tough guy[2]. Bruno hadn't seen him for years and he wasn't sorry.

It's an unfair world we live in, Bruno thought. If you're poor you don't get much education and you've little chance of escaping from this situation. Bruno shivered[3] and quickly thought of something more positive.

He smiled as he thought of his mom and all the other ordinary[4] people who lived in the favela, trying to earn an honest living. Day after day they walked up and down the steep steps into Rio to their low-paid, unskilled jobs. But they always had a smile and a big hello for everyone they met.

When he was about eight years old Bruno asked his mother, "Why do we live here and not down there near the beach in those beautiful apartment blocks[5]?"

"That's just the way things are, dear," his mother replied. "In this world there are rich people and there are poor people, and we are poor. There's no way we could ever live like them."

He did not really understand this at that time.

---

1 crime [kraɪm] (n.) 罪
2 tough guy 惡霸
3 shiver [ˈʃɪvə] (v.) 顫抖
4 ordinary [ˈɔrdn͵ɛrɪ] (a.) 普通的
5 block [blɑk] (n.) 街區
6 tattoo [tæˈtu] (n.) 刺青

7 carpe diem [ˈkɑrpɛ ˈdiɛm]〔拉〕
   抓住今天（=seize the day）
8 profound [prəˈfaʊnd] (a.) 深深的
9 unorthodox [ʌnˈɔrθə͵dɑks] (a.)
   非正統的

Bruno then looked at the inside of his right forearm and the black tattoo[6] he had recently got done there.

Carpe Diem[7] was a quote from his favorite movie, *Dead Poets Society.* He'd seen the movie five years ago and it had had a profound[8] effect on him. The story was about an English teacher, John Keating, in a school for boys. His lessons are unusual and unorthodox[9] and he inspires his students to change their lives and find the courage to do what they want in life. He tells them constantly, "Carpe diem. Seize the day, boys! Make your lives extraordinary!"

Yes! That's it! Bruno thought at the time. Things are not the way they are just because that's the way they are. We *can* change things. We can live the life we want!

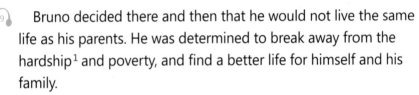

MOVIES

- What is your favorite movie? Why? What is it about?
- Have you ever seen a movie or read a book that has changed your way of thinking?
- Do you think that we can change things and live the life we want? Tell a partner.

Bruno decided there and then that he would not live the same life as his parents. He was determined to break away from the hardship[1] and poverty, and find a better life for himself and his family.

He started to read as much as he possibly could, borrowing books from the local library. He began studying really hard at school, too. And he did very well, getting high grades[2] in all his subjects. But then two years ago, he had to leave school and go to work to help his family. That is when he got this job, selling coconuts at a small kiosk[3] on the beach front in Ipanema.

"Come on, Bruno, I have customers waiting!" his boss shouted, slightly annoyed that Bruno was still sitting on the wall.

"Okay, I'm coming!"

Bruno quickly stopped his daydreaming and jumped up. His break was over. It was time to get back to work.

---

1 hardship [ˈhɑrdʃɪp] (n.) 艱難;困苦
2 grade [gred] (n.) 成績
3 kiosk [kiˈɑsk] (n.) 販賣亭

BRUNO MEETS CLARA

The kiosk where Bruno worked was similar to all the other kiosks that dotted[4] the sidewalk[5] along Ipanema beach. It was a small, square-shaped shop, painted bright red, and conveniently placed between two palm[6] trees that offered a bit of shade. There were a few plastic chairs and tables where customers could sit and chat with friends while they sipped[7] their coconut water.

When Bruno got back there the tables were full and there was a queue[8] of people at the counter[9]. But he was a fast worker and pretty soon all the customers were served. He then went to get some more coconuts from the big refrigerator at the back of the kiosk.

"Hey, you! Give me a coconut water!" someone suddenly shouted rudely[10].

MANNERS

- How do you think Bruno feels?
- Has anyone ever been rude to you? How did you react?

---

4 dot [dɑt] (v.) 星羅棋佈於
5 sidewalk [ˈsaɪdˌwɔk] (n.)〔美〕人行道
6 palm [pɑm] (n.) 棕櫚樹
7 sip [sɪp] (v.) 啜飲

8 queue [kju] (n.) 排成行列
9 counter [ˈkaʊntɚ] (n.) 櫃檯
10 rudely [ˈrudlɪ] (adv.) 無禮地

Bruno was facing the wall so he couldn't see who had spoken. Maybe I'll just pretend I didn't hear anything, he thought to himself. He moved his head to the side to sneak[1] a look at the rude customer. When he saw that it was a beautiful blonde[2] girl he smiled to himself. Then he immediately walked over to the counter.

"Good morning," Bruno said politely, as he smiled winningly[3] at the girl, revealing[4] perfect, pearl-white[5] teeth. But she just ignored[6] his greeting.

"Cut open a fresh coconut for me," she ordered, giving him a bad-tempered[7] scowl[8].

"How much is it?" she continued brusquely[9] without even the slightest sign of a smile on her face.

Bruno served her in his usual efficient way.

She doesn't seem to be very happy. I wonder why. She's so gorgeous[10]! he thought.

He found it odd[11] that so many of these rich young people who went to the kiosks did not seem to be particularly happy. His friends in the favela, who had lots to complain about, were on the whole very cheerful and content[12]. Go figure[13]! Bruno said to himself.

---

1 sneak [snik] (v.) 偷偷地做
2 blonde [blɑnd] (a.)
   白膚金髮碧眼的
3 winningly [ˋwɪnɪŋlɪ] (adv.) 迷人地
4 reveal [rɪˋvil] (v.) 顯露出
5 pearl-white [pɝlˋhwaɪt] (a.)
   像珍珠一樣白的
6 ignore [ɪgˋnor] (v.) 不理會

7 bad-tempered [ˋbædˋtɛmpɚd] (a.)
   脾氣不好的
8 scowl [skaʊl] (n.) 沉下臉；臭臉
9 brusquely [ˋbrʌsklɪ] (adv.) 粗率地
10 gorgeous [ˋgɔrdʒəs] (a.) 很漂亮的
11 odd [ɑd] (a.) 奇怪的
12 content [kənˋtɛnt] (a.) 知足的
13 go figure 搞不懂

MONEY AND HAPPINESS

- Think; then share ideas with a partner.
- Do you need money to be happy? Do you think money can buy you happiness?
- What makes you happy? Write down three things. Share with a partner.

 The girl quickly drank her coconut water, paid and walked away without saying another word. Bruno kept silent, too, while she was there, and just got on with[1] his work. He watched her now as she crossed the road and went into one of the fancy[2] apartment buildings with huge verandas[3], facing the sea, right opposite the kiosk.

I guess that's where she lives, Bruno thought. I wonder what it's like inside. Must be really cool!

"Where have you been, Clara? Wasting your time on the beach again, I'll bet!" her father commented as soon as she entered the living room.

"Hey, leave me alone, will you, dad?"

"You'll never get into university like that! You should be studying hard!"

---

1 get on with sth 進行某件事
2 fancy [ˈfænsɪ] (a.) 別緻的
3 veranda [vəˈrændə] (n.) 廊；陽臺
4 give me a break 讓我休息一下
5 storm off 砰砰碰碰、氣沖沖地離開
6 slam [slæm] (v.) 猛地關上
7 sigh [saɪ] (v.) 嘆息

8 despair [dɪˈspɛr] (n.) 絕望
9 in a bad mood 心情很不好
10 deal with 處理
11 lean [lin] (v.) 倚；靠
12 absorbed [əbˈsɔrbd] (a.) 專注的
13 quizzically [ˈkwɪzɪkəlɪ] (adv.) 疑惑地

"Oh, give me a break[4]!" Clara shouted back as she stormed off[5] into her room and slammed[6] the door behind her. Her father sighed[7] with despair[8]. He could never understand why Clara was always in such a bad mood[9]. All he wanted was the best for his daughter, but he found it difficult to deal with[10] her, especially since her mother died.

MOODS

- Do you ever get into bad moods? When you are in a bad mood, do you treat everybody in the same way? Are you especially hostile towards certain people? Who? Why?
- How can you get out of a bad mood? Make a list with a partner.

Later that day, Bruno was on his own at the kiosk. He was leaning[11] on the counter reading a book, waiting for customers. He was so completely absorbed[12] in his book that he did not notice when Clara arrived. She looked at Bruno quizzically[13] for a moment.

"Oh, I'm sorry! I didn't see you there." Bruno quickly apologized as he suddenly sensed that he was being looked at.

"It's OK. No problem," Clara muttered[1].

"Are you really reading that book, *Captains of the Sand*? It's on the syllabus[2] for the university entrance[3] exams. I should be studying it, but I hate reading. It's so boring. I'd much rather go to the beach or the shopping mall[4]!"

"Hey, this book is really cool, you know!" Bruno replied enthusiastically[5]. "It's about a gang[6] of orphans[7], from seven to fifteen years old—the *captains of the sand*. That's what they used to[8] call abandoned[9] street kids. They live in the streets of Salvador in Bahia, and the only way they can survive[10] is by stealing. I'm reading it for the third time now."

---

1 mutter [ˈmʌtɚ] (v.) 低聲嘀咕
2 syllabus [ˈsɪləbəs] (n.) 課程大綱
3 entrance [ˈɛntrəns] (n.) 入學
4 shopping mall 大型購物中心
5 enthusiastically [ɪnˌθjuzɪˈæstɪklɪ] (adv.) 熱心地
6 gang [gæŋ] (n.) 一幫
7 orphan [ˈɔrfən] (n.) 孤兒

"Yeah, right! Like you're an expert[11] on Brazilian literature[12]!" Clara retorted[13] disbelievingly. "Since when did a guy who sells coconut water waste his time reading literature?"

"Well, do you want to know something? I love reading and I don't think it's a waste of time!"

"No way[14]! You're kidding me[15], right?"

"No, I'm serious. I want to study Portuguese[16] Language and Literature at university. So I'm studying now to pass the entrance exams for a public university. It's free there. My family's poor and I could never afford[17] to go to a private[18] university."

"Wow! That's amazing!" Clara said, finally convinced[19] that Bruno was really telling the truth.

8 used to 以前常常……
9 abandoned [ə'bændənd]
   (a.) 被遺棄的
10 survive [sə'vaɪv] (v.) 活下來
11 expert ['ɛkspət] (n.) 專家
12 literature ['lɪtərətʃə] (n.) 文學
13 retort [rɪ'tɔrt] (v.) 反駁；回嘴

14 no way〔口〕不可能
15 You're kidding me. 你在跟我開玩笑吧。
16 Portuguese ['portʃu‚giz] (n.) 葡萄牙語
17 afford [ə'ford] (v.) 供得起
18 private ['praɪvɪt] (a.) 私立的
19 convince [kən'vɪns] (v.) 說服

There was a brief, awkward[1] silence. Bruno and Clara just looked at each other. Neither of them knew what to say next. Then Bruno broke the silence and asked, "So, what's your name?"

"I'm Clara. And you?"

"Bruno. Hey, Clara. If you want we could meet later and I could try to tell you why this book is so great. What do you think?"

"Hmm, I dunno[2]. My dad is very strict[3]. He doesn't let me stay out late. And I have to go to class later this afternoon. I'm doing one of those crash courses[4] for the university entrance exams. What time do you finish here?"

"Six o'clock."

"OK, I could meet you here at about six fifteen."

"Great! So I'll see you later then." Bruno said, beaming[5] with delight[6].

Clara turned round to walk away, when Bruno suddenly remembered something.

"Hey, Clara," he called after her. "I forgot to give you your coconut water!"

Clara smiled. "No problem! I forgot to ask for one!"

Clara arrived at the kiosk at six fifteen sharp[7]. Bruno had been waiting anxiously all afternoon. He wasn't sure that she would actually turn up[8].

---

1 awkward [ˋɔkwəd] (a.) 笨拙的
2 dunno [ˋdʌnə] (v.) 〔口〕不知道
3 strict [strɪkt] (a.) 嚴格的
4 crash course 速成課
5 beam [bim] (v.) 照耀
6 delight [dɪˋlaɪt] (n.) 愉快
7 sharp [ʃɑrp] (adv.) 整點地
8 turn up 出現

9 stroll [strol] (v.) 散步；蹓躂
10 intrigued [ɪnˋtrigd] (a.) 被迷住的
11 impressed [ɪmˋprɛst] (a.) 受感動的
12 architecture [ˋɑrkə͵tɛktʃə] (n.) 建築
13 It's a deal. 就這麼說定了。
14 Let's shake on it. 握手成交。
15 date [det] (v.) 約會

They strolled[9] along the beach front, chatting about themselves. Then, as promised, Bruno told Clara about the book—*Captains of the Sand*. She listened, intrigued[10] and impressed[11].

"This is amazing", Clara said. "You make it all sound so interesting. My Portuguese teacher at school is so boring. I wish I had a teacher like you. I've always found Portuguese really difficult, especially the literature. I'm good at math and I'm going to study architecture[12] at university. I'm trying to get in to public university, too, as the courses are better. But the entrance exam is really difficult."

"Hey, why don't we give each other a hand? I'll help you with your Portuguese and you can help me with my math. I'm useless at math. So, what do you think?"

"OK, it's a deal[13]!"

Bruno held his hand out and said, "So, let's shake on it[14]."

And they shook hands.

Bruno and Clara started meeting every day and pretty soon, as well as helping each other with their studies. They also started dating[15]. They were both very happy.

SCHOOL

- What is your favorite subject at school?
- What is your least favorite?
- What would you like to do when you finish school?
- Do you and your friends help each other like Bruno and Clara?

BRUNO MEETS CLARA'S FATHER

Clara's dad, Pedro, was a tall, well-dressed, distinguished-looking man. He was fussy[1] and proud of his appearance. He was in his late forties and his hair was starting to go gray at the sides. He was also beginning to lose his hair at the front. Once a month he had his hair cut at a madly expensive hairdressing salon[2], convinced that the more he paid, the less hair would fall out. He had green eyes and wore a pair of expensive glasses which he kept cleaning fastidiously[3] with a cotton handkerchief he always carried in his pocket.

Pedro's father had been an army officer. And although Pedro had never been in the army, he seemed to have inherited[4] his father's highly organized and methodical[5] way of doing everything. He was also very set in his ways[6], with deeply-rooted habits and very strong opinions, often refusing to even consider what other people thought.

APPEARANCES

- Are you fussy about your appearance? How long does it take you to get ready before you go out? Describe your appearance to a partner.

Pedro was an only son and had inherited from his father the family furniture-making business. He was rich and successful but had few real friends. His wife, Clara's mother, had been his only real friend, and when she died of cancer[7] three years ago, Pedro was devastated[8].

After her death he decided to move to the apartment in Ipanema with his only daughter, Clara. He could no longer bear to stay in the house where they had all lived together. There were too many memories there and he wanted to make a new start in life.

Pedro arrived home from work one day, and while he was waiting for the elevator[9] the concierge[10] of the building came up to him, smiled politely and said, "Good evening, Senhor[11] Pedro. I see your daughter's dating now. He looks like a nice, hard-working, young man. You must be happy."

1 fussy ['fʌsɪ] (a.) 挑剔的
2 hairdressing salon 理髮廳
3 fastidiously [fæs'tɪdɪəslɪ] (adv.) 過分講究地
4 inherit [ɪn'hɛrɪt] (v.) 遺傳
5 methodical [mə'θɑdɪkəl] (a.) 講究方法的
6 be set in one's ways 習慣和想法一成不變
7 cancer ['kænsɚ] (n.) 癌症
8 devastated ['dɛvəs,tetɪd] (a.) 身心交瘁的
9 elevator ['ɛlə,vetɚ] (n.) 電梯
10 concierge [,kɑnsɪ'ɛrʒ] (n.) 〔法〕門房
11 senhor [se'njor] (n.) 〔葡〕先生

 But Pedro wasn't happy. He just nodded[1]. The elevator arrived and the concierge held the door open for him. Pedro marched into the elevator, seething[2] with anger.

"Clara!" he shouted as soon as he walked into the apartment. "Where are you?"

"I'm here, dad! Calm down!"

When Clara saw her father's bright red face she knew it was something serious.

"What's the matter, dad?"

"Just answer my question! Are you going out with some guy that I've never even heard about?" he shouted.

"Yes!" replied Clara, firmly[3]. "What's the big deal[4]? I'm not a little kid any more! I'm seventeen years old, dad!"

"Yes, and old enough to get into trouble. You're still my daughter and you do what I tell you, young lady. Don't forget that!"

PARENTS

- What type of relationship does Clara have with her father?
- How do you get on with[5] your parents? Do you tell them everything?
- Who makes the rules in your house?

---

1 nod [nɑd] (v.) 點頭
2 seethe [sið] (v.) 沸騰；激動
3 firmly [ˈfɝmlɪ] (adv.) 堅定地
4 big deal〔俚〕大事情
5 get on with 馬上進行……

6 exasperation [ɪgˌzæspəˈreʃən] (n.) 惱怒；激怒
7 outburst [ˈautˌbɝst] (n.) 爆發
8 sternly [ˈstɝnlɪ] (adv.) 嚴厲地
9 confess [kənˈfɛs] (v.) 坦白；承認

"Come on, dad," Clara sighed in exasperation[6]. She felt a bit calmer now after her little outburst[7].

"Bruno is a really nice guy, and I like him—a lot!"

"So, who is this Bruno guy anyway?" her father asked sternly[8]. He had calmed down, too.

Clara told her dad that she had met Bruno at the kiosk and that he was helping her with her studies so that she could pass the university entrance exams. She didn't mention that Bruno worked at the kiosk and that he lived in the favela. She also confessed[9] to him that the relationship was getting serious.

Pedro listened carefully, then said, "I want to meet him. I'll book a table for the three of us at that nice Italian restaurant on the corner, for eight o'clock tomorrow night. And tell him not to be late. You know how I hate having to wait for people."

Bruno felt a moment of sheer[1] panic[2] when Clara told him that her father wanted to meet him at the restaurant. I don't even have a shirt or tie! he thought. And I can't possibly turn up in shorts and a T-shirt.

Then he thought of Tiago, his neighbor. Tiago always wore a shirt and tie for special occasions and he was about the same size as Bruno. Tiago was only too happy to help Bruno out. He even knotted[3] the tie for him. Bruno had never worn a tie before.

"How can you wear this thing?" Bruno asked his friend, pulling at the collar of his shirt to loosen his tie.

"You'll get used to⁴ it," his friend said, laughing. "Now stop messing about⁵ with the collar."

Bruno's mother came into the room and stood there for a moment, gazing lovingly at her son.

"Goodness gracious! What a handsome young man we have here!"

"Thanks, Mom. I feel so nervous. I really want Clara's dad to like me."

"How could he possibly not like you? Just mind your manners⁶ and don't pretend to be someone you're not. Be yourself. That's who Clara fell for⁷ in the first place, isn't it?" And she gave a chuckle⁸ of delight.

PRETENDING

- What does Bruno's mother mean when she says: "don't pretend to be someone you're not"?
- Have you ever pretended to be different from the way you are?
- Are you the same with everybody that you know?

"Now off you go and enjoy yourself!" she said, giving him a big hug and a kiss.

Bruno rushed out of the room, worried that he might be late.

---

1 sheer [ʃɪr] (a.) 全然的
2 panic [ˋpænɪk] (n.) 恐慌
3 knot [nɑt] (v.) 打結
4 get used to 習慣於
5 mess about 粗暴對待
6 manners [ˋmænɚz] (n.) 〔複〕禮貌；規矩
7 fall for 迷戀
8 chuckle [ˋtʃʌkl̩] (n.) 咯咯笑

At five minutes to eight, Bruno was standing outside the restaurant. He had never been anywhere like this before in his life. Beads[1] of sweat started to roll down his face as he stood petrified[2] between two large marble[3] pillars, staring at the door. Then he took a couple of deep breaths. Okay, here we go, he said to himself and he opened the main door.

His confidence[4] quickly disappeared as soon as he entered the restaurant. He had never seen a place like this before. There were big, sparkling chandeliers[5] hanging from the ceiling and plush[6], deep-pile[7] carpets on the floor. The round tables all had white linen[8] tablecloths and the comfortable, padded[9] chairs were upholstered[10] in deep red satin[11]. Bruno stared at the bewildering[12] array[13] of knives, forks, spoons, plates and glasses on each of the tables.

"Oh, boy, this is not going to be easy!" he thought to himself.

Then he saw Clara rushing towards him. What a relief!

"Hiya! I'm not late, am I?" he asked, as he kissed her quickly on the cheek. He was afraid her dad might not want him to kiss her on the lips.

No, you're right on time. Come on. My dad's over there, waiting to meet you."

She took his hand and led him over to the table, where Pedro was sitting. Pedro stood up, politely introduced himself, and then quickly said, "I've already ordered for all of us. I presume[14] you like your pasta[15] *al dente*[16]?"

1 bead [bid] (n.) (有孔的) 小珠子
2 petrified [ˈpɛtrɪfaɪd] (a.) 驚呆的
3 marble [ˈmɑrbl] (a.) 大理石的
4 confidence [ˈkɑnfədəns] (n.) 信心
5 chandelier [ˌʃændlˈɪr] (n.) 枝形吊燈
6 plush [plʌʃ] (a.) 奢華的
7 pile [paɪl] (n.) 地毯的絨毛
8 linen [ˈlɪnən] (a.) 亞麻布的
9 padded [ˈpædɪd] (a.) 有裝填墊料的
10 upholster [ʌpˈholstɚ] (v.) 裝上墊子

11 satin [ˈsætɪn] (n.) 緞
12 bewildering [bɪˈwɪldərɪŋ] (a.) 迷亂的
13 array [əˈre] (n.) 一系列
14 presume [prɪˈzum] (v.) 假定；設想
15 pasta [ˈpɑstɑ] (n.) 義式麵糰；通心粉
16 al dente [æl ˈdɛntɪ] (a.) 〔義〕有嚼勁的

 "Yes, of course," Bruno answered, not having the slightest idea what *al dente* was, but since it had already been ordered, it did not make any difference.

The atmosphere was tense and strained[1] and Bruno was feeling very uncomfortable with the whole situation.

UNCOMFORTABLE SITUATIONS

- Have you ever been in an uncomfortable situation? Describe it to a partner.
- What did you do?

Pedro was very pleasant at first, but soon the polite conversation turned to more straightforward[2] questions about Bruno's family and his plans for the future.

"What kind of future are you going to offer my daughter?" Pedro asked bluntly[3].

Before Bruno could reply, a middle-aged couple approached[4] their table, calling out, "Pedro, fancy[5] seeing you here! How are you?"

Pedro jumped up with a big smile on his face: it was one of his best customers with his wife. Even though they were not invited, they quickly sat down at Pedro's table and were briefly introduced to Clara and Bruno.

The tense atmosphere immediately became more relaxed. Even Pedro was more talkative and friendly.

Then Carlos, Pedro's customer, smiled at Bruno and asked, "So what do you do, Bruno?"

"I work." Bruno replied, shifting[6] about uneasily on his chair.

"What kind of work?"

"Sales," he continued, not knowing quite what to say.

"A kiosk." Clara chipped in[7], trying to help the conversation run more smoothly.

"Ah, you own a kiosk! Very nice! I believe there's a lot of easy profit there."

"No, I sell coconut water at a kiosk on the beach front," Bruno added.

There was a sudden silence and it felt so tense that you could have cut the air with a knife.

Then, in an instant the bill was paid and they all rapidly went their separate ways.

After that evening, Pedro was convinced that Bruno was not good enough for his daughter, and made it quite clear to her that he was totally against the idea of her dating a mixed-race guy from a completely different background. He told her to stop seeing Bruno and made her stay at home in the evenings to study, on her own.

---

1 strained [strend] (a.) 緊張的
2 straightforward [ˌstretˈfɔrwəd] (a.) 直截了當的
3 bluntly [ˈblʌntlɪ] (adv.) 直率地
4 approach [əˈprotʃ] (v.) 走近
5 fancy [ˈfænsɪ] (v.) 沒想到……
6 shift [ʃɪft] (v.) 挪動
7 chip in 插話

BRUNO AND CLARA

- Do you think Clara's dad is fair?
- Do you think parents should decide who their children date?
- Can you think of any other stories like Bruno and Clara's, where parents tried to stop their children from seeing each other?

Clara, of course, continued to meet Bruno secretly during the day time. And every evening before returning to the favela after work, Bruno waited under her balcony so that she could blow kisses down to him and wave goodbye.

CLARA GOES TO THE FAVELA

Clara had never been to visit Bruno's family in the favela. Her father always kept a close eye on her, especially after that unforgettable dinner at the restaurant. Bruno had invited her many times, and she really wanted to meet his family, specially his mother. She really admired Bruno's mother for bringing up three children on her own, as a poor, single mother.

Then one day, unexpectedly, Pedro announced that he had to go to São Paulo for work for the weekend for a furniture exhibition[1].

He was worried about Clara but she said she would stay with a friend and study. She didn't say that she'd go to Bruno's house, too.

Bruno was delighted when Clara told him that she was going to visit them. He told his mother immediately and she said she would cook one of her famous *feijoadas*[2]. Dona Maria's *feijoada* was said to be the best in the favela, and, probably, in the whole of Brazil.

FOOD

- *Feijoada* is a typical Brazilian dish with beans, salt beef and pork. What are the specialities in your country? What is your favorite food?

Bruno picked Clara up in front of her apartment on Saturday morning and they took a bus to the bottom of the hill where the favela was located. Then they started the long climb up the steep, winding[3] steps.

Clara had tried to prepare herself before coming, but everyone seemed to be even poorer than she had imagined.

As soon as they entered Bruno's house, Dona Maria rushed over to them and threw her arms around Clara, kissing her on both cheeks.

1 exhibition [ˌɛksə'bɪʃən] (n.) 展覽
2 feijoada [ˌfeʒu'ɑdə] (n.)（巴西的招牌菜）以黑豆和各種煙燻乾肉燉煮而成
3 winding ['waɪndɪŋ] (a.) 彎彎曲曲的

 "Welcome to my home, Clara. I'm so happy to meet you. Bruno has told us all about you. Please make yourself at home. It's all very simple here, but you won't go hungry. I'm making my special *feijoada*. And it's nearly ready."

"Thanks, Dona Maria, it's really great to be here and to meet you," Clara said, still a little overwhelmed[1] by everything.

Bruno led[2] her into the living room where she met his younger brother and sister and lots of other relatives and friends who had come as usual for their Saturday lunch. Everyone welcomed Clara with open arms and the atmosphere was so relaxed and friendly that she soon felt as if she had known them all her life.

After lunch everyone moved to the flat, open roof of the house. Musical instruments[3] suddenly appeared from nowhere. Soon everyone was either playing, singing or dancing to the beat[4] of the samba[5]. There were all kinds of drums, and stringed[6] instruments, tambourines[7], shakers[8], scrapers[9], and bells. Bruno picked up a *cuíca*, a drum that makes a high-pitched[10] squeaky[11] noise. Clara laughed in delight and tapped[12] her feet to the rhythm[13].

"I feel so stupid! I don't know how to play anything," she whispered into Bruno's ear, feeling left out[14].

---

1 overwhelmed [ˌovəˈhwɛlmd] (a.) 被震懾住的
2 lead [lid] (v.) 帶領 (動詞三態： lead; led; led)
3 musical instrument 樂器
4 beat [bit] (n.) 拍子
5 samba [ˈsæmbə] (n.) 森巴舞曲
6 stringed [strɪŋd] (a.) 有弦的
7 tambourine [ˌtæmbəˈrin] (n.) 鈴鼓
8 shaker [ˈʃekə] (n.) 手搖鈴
9 scraper [ˈskrepə] (n.) 刮片
10 high-pitched [ˈhaɪˌpɪtʃt] (a.) 高聲調的
11 squeaky [ˈskwikɪ] (a.) 發短促尖聲的
12 tap [tæp] (v.) 輕拍
13 rhythm [ˈrɪðəm] (n.) 節拍；韻律
14 left out 被冷落的

"Of course you do," Bruno said, laughing. "Here you are!" And he gave her a whistle. "Just blow it when you feel like it. You can't go wrong!"

They played, sang and danced the whole afternoon and into the early hours of the evening. Clara couldn't remember the last time that she had enjoyed herself so much.

MUSIC

- What is your favorite type of music? Who are your favorite singers and bands?
- Can you play an instrument? Which one?
- Would you like to be able to play an instrument? Which one?

Clara had often heard about the *baile funk*[1] dance parties that took place[2] in the favelas, but she had never been to one herself. This was her chance to finally go to one, so she asked Bruno if he would take her that evening. She had listened to some of the music at home: funky[3] rhythms with strong rap[4]-style lyrics[5] often about important social issues[6] such as poverty, racism[7], violence[8] and justice[9].

---

1 baile funk 里約特有的舞曲音樂
2 take place 發生
3 funky [ˈfʌŋkɪ] (a.) 放克音樂的
4 rap [ræp] (n.) 饒舌樂
5 lyrics [ˈlɪrɪks] (n.) 〔複〕歌詞

6 issue [ˈɪʃju] (n.) 議題
7 racism [ˈresɪzəm] (n.) 種族主義
8 violence [ˈvaɪələns] (n.) 暴力
9 justice [ˈdʒʌstɪs] (n.) 正義

As they walked towards the dance hall, she felt excited yet also a bit anxious and on edge[10]. Her father would go mad[11] if he ever found out where she was going.

RAP

- The word rap is an acronym[12]. What do the letters R A P stand for?
- Do you like rap? What famous rappers do you know?
- Do you think music can change society? How? With a partner think of songs that have strongly influenced the way people think and act.

When they arrived, the huge dance hall was already packed to capacity[13] with hundreds of young people from the favela. The music was deafeningly[14] loud, and people were dancing like crazy everywhere. Clara felt like a fish out of water[15]. Bruno put his arm around her and held her close to him the whole time, which made her feel warm and protected.

---

10 on edge 緊張的
11 go mad 發瘋
12 acronym [ˋækrənɪm] (n.) 首字母縮略字
13 capacity [kəˋpæsətɪ] (n.) 容量
14 deafeningly [ˋdɛfənɪŋlɪ] (adv.) 震耳欲聾地
15 like a fish out of water 格格不入

After a while, she turned to Bruno and said, "Shall we go? I feel a bit uncomfortable. This really isn't my scene[1]. Do you mind?".

"Of course not," Bruno said, smiling. "It's not my thing[2], either. I didn't think you'd really like it. I just need to go to the bathroom. Stay here and don't move. I'll be right back, OK?"

Clara watched Bruno as he disappeared into the crowd. Soon he was completely out of sight. A split second[3] later, a tall heavy-set[4] man appeared in front of her. He was wearing a tight white T-shirt that showed off his muscular arms.

"What does the bouncer[5] want with me?" Clara thought to herself as she moved away from him.

But the man stepped forward. He was standing so close to her that she could feel his hot, smelly[6] breath on her face.

"Hey, babe! What's a pretty little rich girl like you doing here?"

Clara's heart pounded[7] with fear and she wished with all her heart that Bruno would come back quickly.

FEAR

- Clara is afraid. Imagine you are in her situation. What would you do?
- Think of a time when you felt afraid. What happened? What did you do?
- Make a list of the things you are afraid of. Share with a partner.

"I'm with my boyfriend. He's just gone to the bathroom. He'll be right back any second now." Clara sounded sure of herself but she felt like crying.

The man put his arm around Clara's shoulders. "Aw, come on. Let's have a dance while you're waiting for him," the man insisted with a sleazy[8] smile.

But just then Bruno came running towards him.

"Get your hands off her, Zeca!" Bruno shouted.

Then Bruno suddenly felt a sharp pain in both sides of his head as two guns were pressed violently against his ears by the big guy's bodyguards. Bruno froze[9], paralyzed[10] with fear.

"It's OK!" the man shouted, laughing loudly. "Let him go. He's my friend. Right, Bruno? Hey, man, long time no see, eh? So what's up? I see you've got yourself a nice lady!"

"All's well, man." Bruno replied.

After a few seconds of strained silence, Bruno added, "We've got to go now, OK? So, see you around, right?"

1 not my scene〔口〕不合我的口味；不是我的菜
2 not my thing〔口〕不合我的口味；不是我的菜
3 a split second 一剎那
4 heavy-set [ˈhɛvɪˌsɛt] (a.) 大塊頭的
5 bouncer [ˈbaʊnsɚ] (n.) 龐然大物
6 smelly [ˈsmɛlɪ] (a.) 氣味難聞的
7 pound [paʊnd] (v.) 猛擊
8 sleazy [ˈslizɪ] (a.) 可鄙的
9 freeze [friz] (v.) 驚呆住（動詞三態：freeze; froze; frozen）
10 paralyzed [ˈpærəˌlaɪzd] (a.) 驚呆的

"Yeah, see you, man. You take care now," Zeca said, nodding his head, with a menacing[1] look.

Bruno took a deep breath and gave Clara an apologetic[2] smile. She was shaking with fear. Bruno took her by the hand and they slowly walked away in silence, not daring to look back.

Bruno had a terrible sinking feeling in the pit of his stomach[3]. He knew that he would be seeing Zeca again very soon.

---

1 menacing [ˈmɛnɪsɪŋ] (a.) 險惡的
2 apologetic [əˌpɑləˈdʒɛtɪk] (a.) 道歉的
3 have a sinking feeling in the pit of one's stomach
   有一種不祥之感

ZECA'S EVIL PLAN

José Carlos dos Santos had been given the nickname Zeca when he was just a kid, and it had stuck[4]. He was always much bigger and stronger than the other boys of his age and he often bullied[5] anyone who was smaller and weaker than he was. Soon all the children in the neighborhood were afraid of him, and what Zeca said, ruled.

BULLYING

- Have you ever been bullied? Do you know any bullies?
- With a partner think of ways to stop bullying.

Now that Zeca had grown up he was head and shoulders above everyone else in the area. And he made sure he was stronger, too, spending his afternoons pumping iron[6] at the local gym. Big, tall and muscular: nobody messed with[7] Zeca.

---

4 stick [stɪk] (v.) 停留；固定 (動詞三態：stick; stuck; stuck)
5 bully [ˋbʊlɪ] (v.) 霸凌；欺侮
6 pumping iron 舉重
7 mess with 惹；粗暴對待

Zeca had learned to look after himself at an early age. When he was just eight years old, his father was sent to prison for stealing cars. His mother was hardly ever at home and Zeca had to survive on his own.

He soon turned to petty[1] crime, which quickly escalated[2] into more serious offenses[3] such as mugging[4] and extortion[5]. He was a tough kid and by the age of eighteen he had his own gang of thugs[6] and hoodlums[7].

Zeca put his first gang of thieves together in the favela when he was only thirteen years old. He and his gang also controlled the games of football the boys used to play on a small piece of open land in the favela.

---

1 petty [ˈpɛtɪ] (a.) 小的
2 escalate [ˈɛskə,let] (v.) 使逐步增強
3 offense [əˈfɛns] (n.) 犯法
4 mugging [ˈmʌɡɪŋ] (n.) 〔口〕行兇搶劫
5 extortion [ɪkˈstɔrʃən] (n.) 敲詐；勒索
6 thug [θʌɡ] (n.) 惡棍；暴徒

At that time, Bruno was ten and he often went to watch the older boys play. Everyone dreamed of becoming a famous footballer[8] like Adriano, and getting out of the favela forever.

One day, Zeca's team was a player short[9]. He looked closely and intently[10] for a few moments at all the young spectators[11], who were sitting on the walls around the playing field, waiting for the game to start. Then he fixed his gaze on Bruno and called out, "So, do you want to play or what?"

"Me?" Bruno asked in amazement. He went numb[12]. He could not believe his ears.

"Who do you think I'm talking to?" Zeca shouted, starting to get a bit angry.

---

7 hoodlum [ˈhudləm] (n.) 〔口〕流氓
8 footballer [ˈfutˌbɔlɚ] (n.) 足球運動員
9 short [ʃɔrt] (a.) 短缺的

10 intently [ɪnˈtɛntlɪ] (adv.) 專注地
11 spectator [spɛkˈtetɚ] (n.) 觀眾
12 numb [nʌm] (a.) 驚呆的；發愣的

Bruno jumped up and ran onto the football pitch[1], filled with excitement.

It was a difficult game, and at the end of the first half, Zeca's team were losing 1-0. Bruno had been playing in the fullback[2] position. Just before the second half started, Zeca called Bruno over and said, "I'm going to move you up front[3]. Let's see how good you are." Then he continued threateningly "You'd better score[4] at least two goals[5]. My team never loses. Got it?"

Bruno was terrified, but as soon as the game started again, he forgot about Zeca and focused on winning. He played brilliantly[6] and scored two spectacular[7] goals. Another boy from his team also scored, making the final score 3-1. They had won!

"You're cool, man!" Zeca said to him after the game. "You can come and play for us whenever you want, OK?"

"Thanks, Zeca," Bruno replied, knowing deep inside that this would not be a good idea.

After winning the football game, Bruno also won Zeca's protection in the favela and nobody dared to mess with him. Bruno was grateful[8] for this, but Zeca also wanted him to join his gang of criminals[9], and this was something Bruno definitely did not want.

For a couple of years after this first game, Bruno used to play the odd[10] game of football just to keep in Zeca's good books[11]. He hadn't played a game or seen Zeca for two years, since he started working at the coconut kiosk.

1 pitch [pɪtʃ] (n.) 運動場
2 fullback ['fʊl͵bæk] (n.) 後衛
3 front [frʌnt] (n.) 前鋒
4 score [skor] (v.) 得分
5 goal [gol] (n.) 得分數
6 brilliantly ['brɪljəntlɪ] (adv.) 出色地

Until now. The chance meeting with Zeca at the dance party had left Bruno worried. He knew it was only a matter of time before Zeca would appear again.

Zeca showed up sooner than Bruno had expected. About a week after the dance party, he was coming home from work when two men suddenly stepped out of an alleyway and pushed him up against the wall. They grabbed[12] him by the arms and one of them said, "Zeca wants to see you, now! Come with us."

They dragged[13] him through several streets, and then pushed him down some steps and into a nearby house. Zeca was already there waiting for him. He was sitting on a high stool, whistling to himself.

"Hey, Bruno! How nice of you to come and visit your old friend," he said, smirking[14] sarcastically[15]. "Sit down. You and I have some serious things to talk about."

Zeca then told him all about a foolproof[16] plan he had to steal the official university entrance exams, and sell them before the day of the exam. He had a contact[17] at the company where the exams were printed and he was going to make a copy of the papers for Zeca.

7 spectacular [spɛkˋtækjələ] (a.) 引人注目的
8 grateful [ˋgretfəl] (a.) 感激的
9 criminal [ˋkrɪmən!] (n.) 罪犯
10 odd [ɑd] (a.) 非經常的
11 in one's good books 被某人列在歡迎人物當中
12 grab [græb] (v.) 攫住
13 drag [dræg] (v.) 拖
14 smirk [smɜk] (v.) 嘻嘻作笑
15 sarcastically [sɑrˋkæstɪkəlɪ] (adv.) 挖苦地
16 foolproof [ˋfulˏpruf] (a.) 安全無比的
17 contact [ˋkɑntækt] (n.) 熟人

"Now this is where you come in[1]" he continued to explain. "You and that pretty little rich girlfriend of yours are going to help us sell the results to her friends, all those rich kids in Ipanema. And I'll give you and the girl the papers, too. So you both get into university. That's what you always wanted, isn't it, Bruno?"

BRUNO

- What do you think Bruno is going to do?
- What would you do?
- What advice would you give Bruno?

Bruno sat, speechless. He was in a state of total shock. Before he could collect himself[2], Zeca went on, "Oh, and by the way, just in case you're thinking about pulling a fast one[3] and not helping us, we know where Clara and her dad live. We can pay them a surprise visit any time we want. And I don't think they'd be too happy to see us."

Zeca cackled[4] with laughter while Bruno was led outside, as white as a sheet[5].

---

1 come in 在某事物中起作用
2 collect oneself（震驚之後）恢復過來
3 pull a fast one 從中搞鬼
4 cackle [ˈkækl] (v.) 格格笑
5 as white as a sheet 蒼白如紙

BRUNO'S DILEMMA

Bruno was now facing a real dilemma[6].

On the one hand, he now had a quick way to escape from his dead-end[7] life in the favela. If he helped Zeca to sell the stolen exam results he had a guarantee[8] of a free place at one of the top universities. A sure passport to a better future, and the fast track to wealth and maybe even happiness.

On the other hand, Zeca was asking him to do something illegal[9] and bad. A society needs rules and systems, Bruno thought. If you break the rules and cheat the systems, it's wrong, morally[10] wrong.

Bruno's mother had always tried to teach him the difference between right and wrong, and the importance of keeping on the right side of the law.

But if I don't do what Zeca wants, I'll be putting the lives of Clara and her father seriously at risk, Bruno thought.

Bruno didn't know what to do, torn[11] between doing the right thing and going for the quick fix to his difficult life.

---

6 dilemma [də`lɛmə] (n.) 困境；進退
  兩難
7 dead-end [`dɛd͵ɛnd] (a.) 沒有前途的
8 guarantee [͵gærən`ti] (n.) 保證

9 illegal [ɪ`ligl̩] (a.) 非法的
10 morally [`mɔrəlɪ] (adv.) 道德上地
11 tear [tɛr] (v.) 撕扯 (動詞三態：
   tear; tore; torn)

RIGHT AND WRONG

- Imagine you are in Bruno's situation. What would you do?
- Is there any time when it is possible to justify doing something wrong? If so, when?

 Bruno racked[1] his brains for ways to escape from his predicament[2]. Then he finally decided what to do.

He had not told Clara yet about his meeting with Zeca. He knew she would be terrified. But now it was time to tell her everything that had happened, and explain to her what he was going to do. They met in front of Clara's apartment building. And slowly Bruno told her everything. Then he phoned Zeca.

"OK, Zeca, we'll do it. But first you must promise me that Clara and her dad won't get hurt."

"No problem. You have my word[3]. It's time to get moving[4], Bruno! Come to my place right away. The rest of the gang will be there, too. We'll fill you in on[5] all the details."

Then Zeca gave Bruno directions to a store on one of the street corners in the favela. One of Zeca's men would meet him there and take him to the gang's hideout[6].

---

1 rack [ræk] (v.) 盡力使用
2 predicament [ˌprɪˈdɪkəmənt] (n.) 困境
3 You have my word. 我向你保證。
4 get moving 開始行動吧
5 fill you in on 告知你想要或需要的消息
6 hideout [ˈhaɪdaʊt] (n.) 藏身處

Sure enough a tall, vicious[7]-looking man was waiting for him.

He led Bruno along narrow, winding tracks, up to the highest spot on the hill.

The midday sun was blazing[8] down and Bruno felt he was being watched for the whole journey. He took off his sunglasses to wipe his brow with a handkerchief, but he put them back on again when he saw Zeca and his gang come into sight. They were sitting round a big table in the backyard of a house, playing cards.

"Hey, Bruno! Great to see you, man!" Zeca shouted. "Come over here and meet the boys."

But before Bruno could move he was frisked[9] by two guards.

He cringed[10] as the men searched his body for hidden guns, knives or other weapons.

"He's clean, boss," one of the men shouted out.

Zeca introduced all the members of his gang, including the man who worked inside the printer's who was going to steal the exams. He then explained all the details of the plan. It seemed foolproof. There was no way anything could go wrong.

They all shook hands and quickly left.

Bruno's heart was beating fast. He was anxious to get away from the gang and phone Clara.

---

7 vicious [ˈvɪʃəs] (a.) 邪惡的
8 blaze [blez] (v.) 燃燒；閃耀
9 frisk [frɪsk] (v.) 〔俚〕搜身
10 cringe [krɪndʒ] (v.) 蜷縮

He raced down the hill. Then he stopped at the bottom and looked behind him. It was clear. No one was following him. He took out his phone and called Clara.

"Hey, Clara. Listen." He was out of breath, panting heavily. "Everything went according to plan. To my plan, of course, not Zeca's!" he added, laughing excitedly.

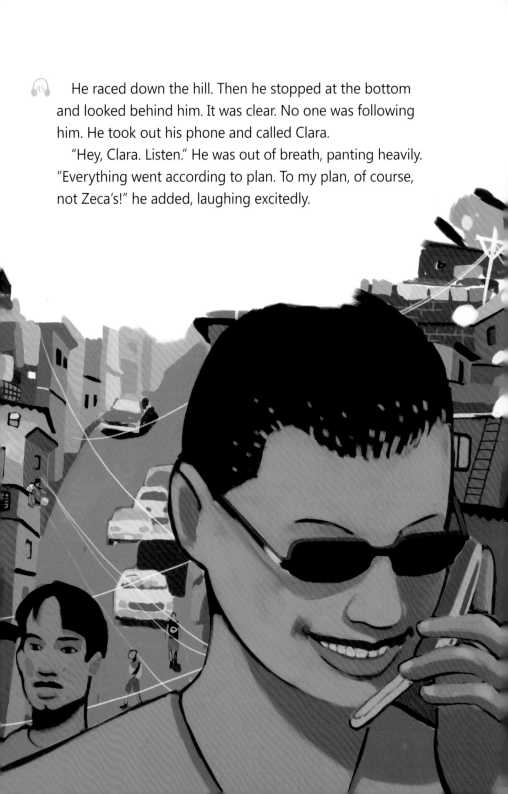

THE ABANDONED FACTORY

"This is amazing!" the police officer said, smiling broadly, as he looked at Bruno and Clara, who were sitting in front of him at the police station. "Well done! How did you manage to come up with such a brilliant idea?"

"Thanks. I guess it was kind of clever." Bruno answered, acknowledging[1] the compliment[2] with a polite smile. He felt slightly embarrassed. "Believe it or not. The idea just popped into my head while I was taking a shower. I remembered I saw an advert[3] once on the Internet for special spy-camera sunglasses. They have a tiny, hidden, built-in[4] video recorder. Here they're only used by detectives[5] and law enforcement agencies[6], but anybody can buy them on the Internet."

When Bruno talked to Clara before his meeting with Zeca's gang, they both agreed it would be wrong to steal the exams, and help Zeca sell them to other people. But Bruno had worked out an ingenious[7] plan to double-cross[8] Zeca and stay out of trouble himself.

---

1 acknowledge [ək`nɑlɪdʒ] (v.) 表示謝忱
2 compliment [`kɑmpləmənt] (n.) 讚美的話；恭維
3 advert [əd`vɝt] (n.) 廣告 (= advertisement)
4 built-in [`bɪlt,ɪn] (a.) 嵌入的
5 detective [dɪ`tɛktɪv] (n.) 偵探
6 law enforcement agency 執法單位
7 ingenious [ɪn`dʒinjəs] (a.) 巧妙的
8 double-cross [`dʌbḷ,krɔs] (v.) 出賣

First of all, he had wisely agreed to go along with[1] Zeca's plan, and go to the meeting with the gang of thieves. When he arrived at the hideout, they frisked him for hidden weapons, but no one ever imagined that Bruno was wearing sunglasses with a tiny built-in camera.

Bruno had secretly videoed the entire meeting, making sure he had taken close-up[2] shots[3] of all the gang members. Their conversations with all the details of their plan had also been recorded.

Then, as soon as he was sure that he wasn't being followed, he phoned Clara and together they went to the police with the camera and told them the whole story.

"Thanks to this evidence[4] we can finally catch Zeca and his entire gang red-handed[5]," the police officer continued. "But we need you and Clara to help us. It's very important that you both continue to act as if nothing has happened. You must play along[6] with whatever Zeca wants. We'll be following your every move from now on. Just do everything Zeca tells you to, OK?"

The police then went to the printer's and spoke to the owner. He agreed to co-operate and they installed[7] some hidden cameras there, too.

The day of the theft they saw the thief copy the exam papers on CCTV[8], but they did not arrest him yet. Then they waited until Zeca made the next move.

Two days later, Bruno was working as usual at the kiosk when his phone rang. It was Zeca. Zeca told him to go with Clara to an old abandoned factory[9] several miles outside of town. The exam papers were ready.

Bruno then called Clara and told her to meet him as soon as possible at the kiosk, so that they could go together. Then he phoned the police to give them the details.

When Bruno and Clara arrived, all the members of the gang were already there waiting for them. They were all laughing and joking, celebrating the success of the theft.

Bruno and Clara joined them and started opening the packets to have a look at the stolen exam papers.

Suddenly the doors crashed[10] open and a loud, firm voice cried out, "Police! Drop your guns! Get down on your knees with your hands above your heads!"

No one heard what was said next as there was a sudden burst[11] of gunfire[12]. People were running all over the place, and clouds of dust flew up from the dirty, old floorboards.

Suddenly a raucous[13] voice yelled out several times, "Hold your fire[14]!"

---

1 go along with 同意；合作
2 close-up [ˋklosˌʌp] (n.) 特寫
3 shot [ʃɑt] (n.) 拍攝
4 evidence [ˋɛvədəns] (n.) 證據
5 red-handed [ˋrɛdˌhændɪd] (a.) 正在作案的
6 play along 合作
7 install [ɪnˋstɔl] (v.) 安裝
8 CCTV 監視攝影機（security camera）
9 factory [ˋfæktərɪ] (n.) 工廠
10 crash [kræʃ] (v.) 發出很響的聲音
11 burst [bɜst] (n.) 爆發
12 gunfire [ˋgʌnˌfaɪr] (n.) 砲火
13 raucous [ˋrɔkəs] (a.) 粗聲的；喧鬧的
14 hold fire 住手

Everyone fell silent. The dust started to settle[1]. Zeca was standing in the middle of the room holding a gun to Clara's head. He screamed out wildly, "Put your guns down and kick them over here! Now lie on the floor—everybody! Or she's dead!"

The police threw down their guns and kicked them towards Zeca. One of the guns bounced[2] across the floor and landed right in front of Bruno, who was kneeling on the floor behind Zeca.

Bruno had no time to think. Almost instinctively[3] he grabbed the gun, aimed it at Zeca's legs and fired. Zeca dropped to the ground. Clara ran towards Bruno.

More armed policemen came rushing in and quickly took control of[4] the situation. Zeca and the rest of the gang were quickly handcuffed[5] and led off to the police cars waiting outside.

Clara fell into Bruno's arms crying and shaking. Neither of them spoke a word. They were both in a state of shock.

COURAGE

- Think of a time when you showed courage.
  Tell a partner what happened and what you did.

---

1 settle [ˈsɛtl̩] (v.) 沈澱下來
2 bounce [baʊns] (v.) 彈起
3 instinctively [ɪnˈstɪŋktɪvlɪ]
   (adv.) 本能地
4 take control of 掌控
5 handcuff [ˈhændˌkʌf] (v.) 戴上手銬

EPILOGUE

One month later

Soon after the police raid[1], Bruno and Clara took the university entrance exams. They both passed and got into the top university.

The authorities[2] were very grateful to Bruno and Clara for stopping the theft and sale of the exams. As well as a full scholarship[3], they both received a very generous grant[4] from the government to cover all their living expenses for the four years of their courses.

On Saturday, Clara's dad, Pedro, organized a celebration lunch at his apartment. Bruno was standing alone on the balcony, gazing out to sea, when Pedro came and stood beside him.

He smiled nervously at Bruno and said, "Look, Bruno. I really want to apologize. When I first met you, I thought you weren't good enough for my daughter. But now I can assure you that I'm glad you had the courage to follow your heart. You saved her life! I can never repay you for that. Please forgive me." Pedro looked at Bruno with tears welling[5] in his eyes.

1 raid [red] (n.) 突襲；襲擊
2 authorities [əˋθɔrətɪz] (n.) 當局
3 scholarship [ˋskɑlɚ͵ʃɪp] (n.) 〔複〕獎學金
4 grant [grænt] (n.) 獎學金
5 well [wɛl] (v.) 湧出

FORGIVENESS

- If you were Bruno, would you forgive Pedro?
- Think of a time when you forgave someone.
  Now think of a time when someone forgave you.

 "Of course I forgive you." Bruno said, smiling warmly. "It was a difficult time for all of us, but all's well that ends well[1], right?"

They hugged each other without saying anything. Then Bruno broke the silence.

"I wonder if lunch is ready," he said. "I'm starving!"

Then a happy, singsong[2] voice called out from the kitchen.

"Come on, everybody!" Dona Maria proudly announced.

"You know something, Bruno." Pedro said in a loud voice. "Your mom's *feijoada* beats pasta *al dente* any day!"

They all burst out[3] laughing as they rushed into the dining room.

---

1 All's well that ends well. 結局好，就一切都好。
2 singsong [ˈsɪŋˌsɔŋ] (a.) 有韻感的
3 burst out 突然……起來 (後接動名詞)

AFTER READING

❹ Personal Response

1 Did you like the story? Why/why not?

2 Could this story take place in your country? If not, why not?

3 Which part of the story did you enjoy most? Explain why.

4 What did you think about Bruno's plan? Would you do the same in his situation?

5 Is there anything you would like to change in the story? Give details.

6 Do you think there are any messages in this story? What are they?

7 Did you like the ending of the story? Did you find it surprising? What did you think would happen?

8 Suggest other ways in which the story could end.

9 Imagine you are making a film of the story. Which famous actors would you choose to play the major roles? What theme song or music would you choose for the film?

Ⓑ Comprehension

10 Tick T (true), F (false) or D (doesn't say).

T F D ⓐ Bruno is the owner of a kiosk in Ipanema.

T F D ⓑ Bruno really likes Brazilian literature.

T F D ⓒ Clara had a rich boyfriend before she met Bruno.

T F D ⓓ Clara's mother died suddenly and unexpectedly of cancer.

T F D ⓔ Clara's dad, Pedro, meets Bruno for the first time at an Italian restaurant.

T F D ⓕ Bruno always wears a collar and tie.

T F D ⓖ Dona Maria, Bruno's mother, makes Clara feel really welcome when she visits their home in the favela.

T F D ⓗ Zeca only thought of stealing the exams after he met Bruno and Clara at the dance hall.

T F D ⓘ Bruno has played football regularly for Zeca's team since he was 12 years old.

T F D ⓙ Bruno agrees to take part in Zeca's plan, but he does not really intend to help him sell the stolen exams.

T F D ⓚ Zeca is shot and dies during the police raid.

T F D ⓛ Bruno and Clara get married before they start their university course.

11 Answer the questions.

ⓐ Why did Bruno have the tattoo *Carpe Diem* on his right forearm?

ⓑ Why was Clara so happy when her father had to travel to São Paulo to go to an exhibition?

ⓒ Why did Bruno agree at first to go along with Zeca's scheme? What did he really plan to do?

12 Write a 150-word summary of the story, but deliberately include 3 incorrect pieces of information. Exchange with a partner and try to discover the mistakes.

13 Write a 150-word summary, but with the sentences mixed up or cut up on separate pieces of paper. Exchange with a partner and try to put the sentences in the correct order.

14 In pairs, write three questions about the story. Then exchange with another pair and answer each other's questions.

15 Match the first part of the sentence from the story to the second part.

_____	a	This was the day Bruno's life
_____	b	We can live
_____	c	Just mind
_____	d	Bruno was feeling very uncomfortable
_____	e	What kind of future are you going
_____	f	It's all very simple here,
_____	g	How nice of you to come
_____	h	You and I have some serious things
_____	i	Put your guns down
_____	j	I'm glad you had the courage

1 to offer my daughter?
2 with the whole situation.
3 to talk about.
4 the life we want.
5 was going to change forever.
6 to follow your heart.
7 and kick them over here.
8 but you won't go hungry.
9 and visit your old friend.
10 your manners.

16 When did the sentences occur in the story? Discuss with a partner.

C Characters

17 Who is speaking? Who are they talking to? What is the situation?

a) Yeah, right! Like you're an expert on Brazilian literature.

b) Get your hands off her!

c) That's just the way things are, dear. In this world there are rich people and there are poor people, and we are poor.

d) I feel so stupid! I don't know how to play anything.

e) You'd better score at least two goals. My team never loses. Got it?

f) If you want we could meet later and I could try to tell you why this book is so great.

g) You saved her life. I can never repay you for that. Please forgive me.

h) What's a pretty little rich girl like you doing here?

i) Are you going out with some guy I've never even heard about?

j) Everything went according to plan. To my plan, of course, not Zeca's!

18 The words and phrases below are used in the story to describe four characters. Put them in the correct columns. One is used twice.

heavy-set
dark brown eyes
blonde hair
smelly breath
distinguished-looking
in his late forties
hair turning gray at the sides

jet-black hair
beautiful
muscular
good-looking
cheerful
young

well-dressed
big
fair-skinned
slim
gorgeous
tall

Bruno

Clara

Zeca

Pedro

19 Who is your favorite character? Explain why.

20 Find examples of words or actions in the story that illustrate the following. Discuss them with your partner.

a Clara is hostile towards her father and argues with him.

b Bruno is brave.

c Clara's father is concerned about his daughter's welfare.

d Bruno's mother is kind and loving.

e Zeca is cruel and threatening.

f Bruno is enthusiastic and hard-working.

g Clara's father worries too much about details and standards.

h Bruno is honest.

i Zeca is the leader of a criminal gang.

j Bruno's mother is a good cook.

D Plot and Theme

21 Put these events from the story in the correct order.

_____ a) Zeca annoyed Clara when she was on her own at the dance party.

_____ b) Bruno met Clara when she went to the kiosk to buy coconut water.

_____ c) Bruno and Clara started dating.

_____ d) Zeca "invited" Bruno to take part in his plan to steal and sell exams.

___1___ e) Bruno saw a movie called *Dead Poets Society* which profoundly impressed him.

_____ f) Bruno and Clara passed the university entrance exams and also got a full scholarship and a grant.

_____ g) Bruno took Clara to a *baile funk* dance party in the favela.

_____ h) Bruno met Clara's father in a posh restaurant.

_____ i) Bruno got his first job selling coconuts and coconut water at a small kiosk in Ipanema.

_____ j) Zeca and his gang were arrested.

_____ k) Clara went to the favela to meet Bruno's family.

_____ l) Zeca's bodyguards took Bruno to see him.

_____ m) Bruno went to the police with recorded evidence of the plan.

22 Listen and check your answers.

23 Make a list of the places that are mentioned in the story. Why are they important?

24 For a story to be plausible (= likely to be true) factual information must be accurate. Find examples of specific details in the story which are realistic and authentic.

25 Write a short summary of the basic plot of the story. Use linking words like the ones below to connect your text. You can use exercise **21** to help you.

after a very short time	soon after	but	soon
the following day	after that	so	finally
then one day	as soon as	then	next
two days / one week etc. later	sometime later	first	

26 What ideas or messages are there in the story? Give examples to support your answer. Below are a few suggestions to help you start.

  a We are responsible for our own lives, and we can change things.

  b Dating people of different races and from different backgrounds is perfectly acceptable.

  c It is important to have clear principles about what is right and wrong.

27 Write a short summary of the events in the story by retelling it from the point of view of one of the characters.

E Language

28 Complete the dialogues with the sentences below.

1. Great! So I'll see you later then.
2. Of course not.
3. No way! You're kidding me, right?
4. No, you're right on time.
5. Oh, give me a break!
6. So, let's shake on it!
7. Okay, I'm coming!
8. I work.
9. I'm here, dad! Calm down!
10. It's OK. No problem.

a. **A** Come on, Bruno, I have customers waiting!
   B

b. **A** You should be studying hard!
   B

c. **A** Oh, I'm sorry! I didn't see you there.
   B

d. **A** I love reading and I don't think it's a waste of time!
   B

e. **A** I could meet you here at about six fifteen.
   B

f. **A** OK, it's a deal!
   B

g. **A** Where are you?
   B

h. **A** Hiya! I'm not late, am I?
   B

i. **A** So what do you do, Bruno?
   B

j. **A** Do you mind?
   B

29 Choose the correct alternative to fill in the spaces in the sentences. Write 1, 2 or 3 in the space.

a Here they're only _____ detectives and law enforcement agencies, but anybody can buy them on the Internet.

① used by   ② use for   ③ using by

b "You'll _____ it," his friend said, laughing. "Now stop messing about with the collar."

① get use to   ② get using to   ③ get used to

c That's what they _____ abandoned street kids in the past.

① usually to call   ② are use to calling   ③ used to call

d He and his gang also controlled the games of football the boys _____ on a small piece of open land in the favela.

① usually play   ② used to play   ③ were used playing

30 Match the adjectives on the left with the nouns on the right to produce the most natural-sounding combination. Make sentences with the words.

_____	a	foolproof	1	mood
_____	b	sheer	2	track
_____	c	first	3	second
_____	d	menacing	4	steps
_____	e	fast	5	panic
_____	f	bad	6	smile
_____	g	stabbing	7	idea
_____	h	split	8	plan
_____	i	broad	9	impression
_____	j	steep	10	look
_____	k	awkward	11	pain
_____	l	brilliant	12	silence

1 Tick T (True) or F (False).

T F   a)   Bruno lived in an apartment block near Ipanema beach.

T F   b)   A film called *Carpe Diem* opened Bruno's eyes to new ways of thinking.

T F   c)   Clara and Bruno met for the first time at a kiosk on the beach front.

T F   d)   Clara and Bruno helped each other to study for the university entrance exams.

T F   e)   Bruno wanted to study math at university.

T F   f)   Pedro found it difficult to deal with Clara after her mother died.

T F   g)   Pedro was very happy when he found out that Clara was dating Bruno.

T F   h)   Bruno arrived late at the restaurant when he went to meet Pedro for the first time.

T F   i)   Bruno's mother was a single mother with three children.

T F   j)   Clara had a wonderful time at the dance party.

T F   k)   Zeca planned to steal the university entrance exams and use Bruno and Clara to sell them.

T F   l)   Bruno secretly videoed the gang of thieves and took the evidence to the police.

T F   m)   All the thieves were killed in the police raid.

T F   n)   Bruno and Clara passed the university entrance exams.

T F   o)   Bruno, Clara and their families organized a celebration party in the favela.

2 With a partner correct the false sentences.

3 Read the text below and choose the correct word for each space. Write 1, 2, or 3 in the space.

Bruno was slim and good-looking with (a) _____, jet-black hair and sparkling, dark brown (b) _____. He had a very distinctive, (c) _____ voice. That was also pleasant and cheerful and warm. But he didn't use his voice to win (d) _____ over. No, whenever Bruno (e) _____ anything, it was always relevant and meaningful. His classmates at school teased him about being (f) _____, but Bruno never got embarrassed or nervous; it was just the way he was. He kept himself to (g) _____.

He only spoke when he had something to say. Oh, and he had one of those irresistible smiles that light up your day. And he constantly looked on the (h) _____ side of things and was optimistic (i) _____ everything. Quite (j) _____, he was a nice happy guy and you couldn't help but like him.

a ① short	② low	③ small
b ① eyelashes	② eyelids	③ eyes
c ① steep	② deep	③ big
d ① people	② persons	③ peoples
e ① spoke	② talked	③ said
f ① shy	② rude	③ genuine
g ① him	② his self	③ himself
h ① bright	② light	③ cool
i ① with	② by	③ about
j ① surely	② simply	③ actually

1 Favelas

a) According to the United Nations, in Brazil between 20% and 30% of the urban population live in favelas. With a partner, research the subject of favelas in Brazil on the Internet. Then tell the class.

For suggestions check the links on the Helbling Readers website.

b) Write a short, personal account about life in a favela from the point of view of one of the people living there.

2 Cyber-bullying

Wikipedia explains that cyber-bullying "involves the use of information and communication technologies to support deliberate, repeated, and hostile behavior by an individual or group, that is intended to harm others."

With a partner research the subject of cyber-bullying on the Internet. Compare this to traditional bullying. Find out about the dangers of this kind of bullying and suggest some possible solutions. Then tell the class.

作者簡介

傑克，跟我們介紹一下你自己吧！

我出生於英國北部，在利物浦大學修德文和俄文。大學畢業後，我花了幾年的時間環遊世界，途中以教英語來打點旅遊的盤纏。我回到英國後，進入倫敦大學的研究所繼續深造。1976 年，我來到了巴西，從此在這裡落腳，以教書和寫作維生。

你是在什麼時候開始寫小說的？

我的第一篇小說於 1999 年出版，而本書是我的第十本著作。

你的故事靈感是怎麼來的？

在我們的身邊，隨時都有故事在發生，這些故事「乞求」我們把它們寫下來，只是我們往往視而不見。我不會刻意去尋找故事，而是這些故事主動找上門的。我的靈感通常是來自真實的事件。

在這篇故事裡，你想要傳達什麼樣的訊息？

這篇故事傳達了許多訊息，而其中最主要的訊息，可以用電影《春風化雨》中那位英文老師的話來做總結——「抓住當下，創造你自己不平凡的人生！」我們可以改變事物，我們可以活出自己所想要的人生，將自己的潛能發揮得淋漓盡致。

你未來是否有計畫再寫什麼其他的故事？

當然，我有一個檔案，裡頭塞滿了各種故事的構想。

布魯諾

P.11

　　布魯諾暫時停下手邊的工作，他坐在海灘前面的一道矮牆上，望著前方的大海。他的臉上掛著微笑，享受片刻的休息，悠遊在思緒裡。

　　今天的天氣又悶又熱，這是里約熱內盧典型的盛夏日子。現在才上午十一點，氣溫就已經飆到三十五度，濕度達到百分之八十二。布魯諾和往常一樣，穿了一件五顏六色、長度及膝的百慕達運動褲，和一件白色的背心，腳上踩著藍色的夾腳拖鞋。陣陣微風正從溫暖的海上吹來，輕拂過他臉上光滑的古銅色肌膚，好不愜意。

　　今天這一天，將是布魯諾人生上的一大轉折。

　　一群女孩走過布魯諾的身邊，對他笑了笑。布魯諾身材修長、臉蛋姣好，有一頭烏黑的短髮和一雙閃爍的深色眸子。布魯諾不只長得帥，而且個性也很好。他的嗓音低沉而獨特，聽起來悅耳、快活又溫暖，而且他講話很中肯實在，不會用語言來迷惑別人。

P.14

　　在學校讀書時，同學會取笑他太害羞，但他不以為意，只是忠於自己的樣子。他是個獨行俠，不喜歡言不及義的閒聊。喔，還有，他的笑容可真令人難以抗拒，看了能讓人一整天都好心情。他凡事樂觀，看什麼事情都很正面。他是一個個性很好的陽光男孩，人見人愛，就這麼簡單。

　　布魯諾靜靜地望著伊帕尼瑪海灘上穿梭的人們，這個海灘上隨處可見光鮮亮麗的有錢人，其中大部分是當地的巴西人，另外也有不少的富人觀光客。沙灘上有衝浪的人，有做日光浴的人，還有幾票人在玩足球、沙灘排球和足排球。足排球結合了足球和排球，它的發源地就在巴西。

　　布魯諾望向右邊遠方的兩座山，那是「兩兄弟山」。里約真是一個人間天堂，他心想著。

巴西

- 你對巴西有何認識？想想看，並和夥伴分享。
- 你的國家以什麼聞名於世界？有哪些觀光景點？

P.15

接著，他環顧四周，看著沿著海灘林立的精緻高樓大廈。在里約，伊帕尼瑪區是生活費最高的頂級住宅區，然而，布魯諾這時所想到的，是自己居住的地方。他住在一處叫做坎榻的貧民區裡，那裡就位在這些昂貴公寓後方的山丘上。

他腦海裡浮現出貧民區的畫面：幾百間狹小破爛、緊緊相挨的茅舍，在半山腰上任意搭建。他想著，那裡住著成千上萬的窮苦人家，人們在交錯複雜的陡峭階梯和通道上，上上下下，巷子很小，彎彎曲曲的，車子要是開進去會險象環生。

P.16

貧民區裡的生活並不好過，年輕人往往會走上為非作歹的路。布魯諾不禁想到了札加。札加從八歲時就開始偷竊，而現在已經是橫行鄰里間的惡霸了。布魯諾有好些年沒見過他，但他並不覺得遺憾。

人類居住的這個世界是不公平的，布魯諾心想。窮人沒有錢接受教育，要從貧困中翻身的機會也就很少，一想到這裡，布魯諾不禁打了個冷顫，於是趕緊把念頭轉掉。

他想到住在貧民區裡的媽媽和其他平凡的人們，他們靠自己的雙手生活，他不禁笑了起來。他們日復一日在陡峭的通道上往返，去里約打雜活，賺取微薄的收入，而且總是笑臉迎人，在路上遇到誰都會打招呼。

布魯諾在八歲時問過媽媽說：「我們為什麼要住在這裡，為什麼不搬到山下，去住海邊那些漂亮的公寓？」

「親愛的，人生就是這樣，」媽媽回答道：「這世界上有窮人、有富人，而我們剛好就是窮人，所以無法過有錢人的生活。」

他當時聽不懂媽媽的回答。

P.17

接著，布魯諾看著自己右上臂內側的黑色刺青，那是他最近才刺上去的。

「抓住當下」這幾個字，是來自他最喜歡的那部電影《春風化雨》。布魯

諾在五年前看過這部電影，讓他感觸很深。故事是講一位名叫約翰・基亭的英國教師在學校教育學子的故事，他教育學生的方法很不一樣，也非常標新主義。他激發學生去改變自己的人生，尋找勇氣去追求自己的人生夢想。他不斷地告訴學生：「孩子們，你們要 Carpe diem，抓住當下，創造你自己不平凡的人生！」

沒錯，就是這樣！這時布魯諾看完電影後的想法。現狀並非是不可改變的，人們可以做出改變，活出自己想要的人生。

P. 18

電影

・你最喜歡的電影是哪一部？為什麼？電影裡在演什麼？

・是否有哪部電影或哪本書，改變了你的某種想法？

・你覺得我們可以做出改變，活出自己想要的人生嗎？和夥伴分享你的想法。

從那時候開始，布魯諾就決定自己以後不要過像父母親那樣的生活。他立志要擺脫艱困和貧窮，為自己和家人開創更好的生活。

他開始去地方圖書館借書，他大量閱讀，在學校上課也很認真，成績因此很優異，每個科目都得到很高的分數。然而在兩年前，他為了幫忙分擔家計，只得輟學工作，在伊帕尼瑪海灘賣椰子汁的攤位上打工。

「布魯諾，快回來，客人都在等啦！」老闆高聲叫道。他看到布魯諾還坐在牆上，有點火大。

「好！我這就來！」

布魯諾中斷他的白日夢，他一躍而起，休息時間已經結束，該回去幹活了。

和克蕾若的邂逅

P. 19

布魯諾打工的販賣亭，就一如其他點綴在伊帕尼瑪海灘人行道上的販賣亭，他的販賣亭小小的，呈四方形，漆成鮮艷的紅色，坐落在兩棵棕櫚樹之間，有一點樹蔭可以遮陽，很便利。販賣亭擺了幾張塑膠桌椅，客人可以坐在那裡，一邊啜飲椰子汁、一邊和朋友閒聊。

布魯諾走回販賣亭時，桌椅上都坐滿了人，櫃檯旁排了一列客人。布魯諾的動作乾淨俐落，沒一會兒就把客人都招呼好了。接著他走到販賣亭後方，從大冰箱裡拿出更多的椰子。

這時傳來一個聲音，沒好氣地喊道：「喂，你，給我一杯椰子汁！」

態度

- 你覺得布魯諾這時作何感受？
- 有人曾經對你很粗魯過嗎？你當時是如何回應的？

P.21

布魯諾面對著牆，看不到講話的人。他心想：我也許應該裝做沒有聽到！他側了一下頭，偷瞄了一眼那位粗魯的客人。當他看到那是一位漂亮的金髮女孩時，不由得笑了出來，立刻來到櫃檯邊。

「早啊！」布魯諾彬彬有禮地說道，對女孩作出燦爛迷人的笑容，露出一口潔白的貝齒，但女孩沒有回應他的問候。

「幫我剖一個新鮮的椰子！」她擺著一張臭臉，指使道。

「多少錢？」她繼續粗魯地問，臉上沒有半點笑容。

布魯諾一如往常熟練地遞上椰子汁。

她看起來心情不是很好，不知道發生了什麼事。她真漂亮啊，他心想。

他發現一件很奇怪的事，上門的顧客中有很多都是有錢的年輕人，然而他們看起來都不是特別開心。反觀他那些貧民區的朋友，雖然生活中可以抱怨的事情一大堆，但他們大體來說都很快活、很知足。怎麼會這樣？布魯諾自言自語道。

P.22

財富與幸福

- 財富和幸福，各是什麼？和夥伴分享你的觀點。
- 你覺得有錢才會幸福嗎？你覺得金錢可以買到幸福嗎？
- 有哪些事情會讓你感到快樂？請寫下三樣，並和夥伴分享你的想法。

女孩很快喝完椰子汁，然後付完錢，吭都沒吭一聲就走了。她還在販賣亭時，布魯諾只是靜靜地繼續忙著手上的工作。在女孩離開時，布魯諾目送她穿過馬路，看見她走進氣派的公寓大樓裡。這座公寓就位在布魯諾的販賣亭正對面，公寓正對著大海，有寬敞的大陽台。

布魯諾心想，我猜她應該就住在公寓裡。公寓裡頭不知長得什麼樣子，一定很炫！

「克蕾若，你野到哪裡去了？你一定又跑去海邊鬼混了！」她前腳才踏進客廳，爸爸便劈頭說道。

「爸，你可以別管我嗎？」

「你這樣怎麼上得了大學，你要用功念書才行！」

P.23

「噢，饒了我吧！」克蕾若一邊回嘴，一邊砰砰碰碰地走進房間，把門甩上。

做父親的心灰意冷地嘆了口氣，他不知道克蕾若為什麼老是心情不好。他只是想把最好的都給女兒，但他不知怎麼和女兒相處，尤其是在她媽媽過世之後。

心情

- 你有時會心情很差嗎？你心情很差時，對待別人的態度會一樣嗎？你對待某些人的態度會特別差嗎？那是什麼人？為什麼會這樣？
- 你心情不好時，會做什麼事來排解？和夥伴把方法列出來。

那天稍晚時，販賣亭裡只有布魯諾一個人，他倚在櫃檯上看著書，一邊等顧客上門。他看書看得入迷，沒發現克蕾若走了過來。她用疑惑的眼神盯著布魯諾好一會兒。

P.24

「噢，抱歉，我沒看到你！」布魯諾意識到有人正瞅著自己猛瞧時，立刻道歉道。

「沒事！」克蕾若喃喃說道。

「你真的在看《沙地隊長》這本書？這是大學入學測驗的必讀書本，我現在也應該要讀的，但我討厭看書，那太無聊了，我寧願去海邊玩或是去賣場逛。」

「嘿，這本書很好看耶！」布魯諾熱切地說道：「這本書講一群七到十五歲的孤兒的故事，這些孤兒就是所謂的沙地隊長。沙地隊長原本是指街頭的流浪兒。這些孤兒住在巴伊亞的薩爾瓦多，靠偷竊為生。這本書我已經在看第三遍了。」

「是嗎？你好像很熟巴西文學！」克蕾若有點不太相信地説道：「從什麼時候開始，連賣椰子的傢伙也會浪費大好時光在讀文學了？」

「你知道嗎，我很喜歡看書，我不覺得看書是在浪費時間。」

「不會吧，你是開玩笑的吧？」

「不，我是説真的。我想上大學修葡萄牙語文學，所以現在在準備公立大學的入學考試。公立大學是免費的，我家很窮，讀不起私立大學。」

「哇，真讓人跌破眼鏡。」克蕾若最後相信了布魯諾的話。

接著是一陣尷尬的沉默，他們彼此對望著，不知道怎麼接話下去。後來，布魯諾打破沉默問道：「你叫什麼名字？」

「我叫克蕾若，你呢？」

「我叫布魯諾，你好，克蕾若。如果我們晚一點可以碰面，我可以再跟你介紹這本書到底好在哪裡，你覺得怎樣？」

「這很難説，我爸管得很嚴，我不可以在外面待得太晚，而且我今天下午有上課，是大學聯考的衝刺班。你什麼時候下班？」

「六點。」

「那好，我六點十五分左右來這裡找你。」

「太好了，那麼到時候見了。」布魯諾眉飛色舞地説道。

等克蕾若轉身離開後，布魯諾突然才想起了什麼。

「喂，克蕾若。」他在後面大聲叫道：「你叫的椰子汁，我忘記拿給你了。」

克蕾若笑了起來，説：「沒關係，我也忘了要點椰子汁。」

六點十五分整，克蕾若來到了販賣亭，布魯諾整個下午都在期待著這一刻，他不確定克蕾若是否會如期出現。

他們沿著海灘散步，聊著彼此的事。隨後，布魯諾依約跟克蕾若講述了《沙地隊長》的內容。克蕾若聽得津津有味。

「真是奇怪，聽你講就有趣，聽我們學校的葡萄牙文老師講就好無聊，真希望我們老師也能像你這樣會講。我一直覺得葡萄牙文很難，尤其是葡萄牙語文學。我的數學比較好，我上大學後想讀建築。我也想進公立大學，那裡的課程比較好，但是入學考試好難喔。」克蕾若説。

「嘿，那我們可以互相幫忙啊！我教你葡萄牙語，你教我數學，我的數學不好。你覺得如何？」

「好啊，就這麼説定了。」

布魯諾伸出手，説道：「那我們就握個手、一言為定吧。」

於是他們握了握手。

就這樣，布魯諾和克蕾若很快就開始每天碰面，互相幫對方補課，而且兩個人也開始了約會，小倆口相處得很甜蜜。

學校

- 你在學校最喜歡的科目是什麼？
- 最不喜歡的科目又是什麼？
- 你畢業之後想要從事什麼樣的工作？
- 你和朋友會像布魯諾和克蕾若那樣互相幫忙嗎？

和克蕾若的爸爸見面

P.28

克蕾若的父親名叫佩卓，他個子高大，很講究自己的穿著，樣子很體面。他很在意自己的外表，而且對自己的外表感到很驕傲。他年近五十，兩邊的鬢角已經開始花白，額前的髮際也愈來愈高。他每個月都會去貴得嚇死人的髮廊理髮，他相信，只要多付一點錢，就可以少掉一些頭髮。他的眸子是綠色的，戴著一副昂貴的眼鏡，他的口袋裡都會有一條棉質手帕，他會不時掏出來，小心翼翼地把眼鏡擦得晶亮。

佩卓的父親是一位軍官，雖然佩卓沒有當過兵，但他大概是繼承了父親的行事風格，做事很有組織，做每件事都很講求方法。他的想法和作法也是一成不變，習慣根深蒂固，而且極為主觀，別人的想法他往往連考慮都不考慮。

外表

- 你會對自己的外表很挑剔嗎？你在出門之前會花多久的時間打點自己的外表？向夥伴描述你的外表。

P.29

佩卓是獨子，從父親手中繼承了家具製造這個家族事業。他財力雄厚，事業做得很成功，但卻沒有幾個真正的朋友。他的妻子，也就是克蕾若的母親，可以說是他唯一真正的朋友，因此當妻子三年前因癌症過世後，佩卓就整個崩潰了。

妻子去世後，佩卓決定帶著唯一的女兒克蕾若搬到伊帕尼瑪區的這棟公寓裡，他無法再待在一家三口生活過的住處，那裡充滿太多的回憶，他想讓自己的生活有一個新的開始。

這天，佩卓下班回家，他在等電梯時，大樓管理員迎面而來，禮貌地向他笑了笑，說道：「晚安，佩卓先生。我看到令媛正在約會，對方的人看起來很不錯，是一個勤奮的年輕人，你一定很高興吧。」

P.30

但佩卓一點也高興不起來，他只是點了點頭。這時電梯剛好打開，大樓管理員連忙為他把電梯的門頂開，佩卓走進電梯，一肚子火冒上來。

「克蕾若，你在哪裡？」他一踏進家門，便大聲喊道。

「爸，我在這裡，別那麼激動！」

克蕾若看到父親一臉漲得通紅，就知道大事不妙了。

「爸，怎麼啦？」

「快回答我！你是不是和一個我聽都沒聽過的男人在約會？」他鬼吼鬼叫起來。

「是啊！」克蕾若語氣堅定地說：「這有什麼好大驚小怪的，我又不是三歲小孩，爸，我都十七歲啦。」

「是的，你大到可以出去惹麻煩了嗎？你是我的女兒，要聽我的話，年輕的小姐，別忘了這點！」

父母親

- 克蕾若和父親的關係如何？
- 你和父母親相處得如何？你會什麼事都跟他們講嗎？
- 你家的規矩誰說了算？

P.31

「爸，拜託！」克蕾若氣憤地嘆了口氣。在一陣宣洩之後，她覺得冷靜了些。

「布魯諾是一個很好的人，我很喜歡他！」

「布魯諾到底是誰？」父親一臉嚴肅地問道。這時他也冷靜了下來。

克蕾若跟爸爸解釋道，她在販賣亭認識布魯諾，布魯諾幫她復習功課、準備大學聯考。不過，她並沒有說布魯諾在販賣亭打工，而且住在貧民區。她也跟爸爸說，他們的交往是很認真的。

P.32

佩卓仔細地聽著，然後說道：「我想見見這個人。我會在街角那家高級義大利餐廳幫我們三個人訂位，就訂明天晚上八點，你要他別遲到，你知道我最討厭等人了。」

當克蕾若說她爸想約他在餐廳裡見面時，布魯諾感到一陣恐慌。他心想，我連一件襯衫或一條領帶都沒有，我總不能穿短褲和 T 袖上陣吧？

這時他想到了狄亞哥。狄亞哥是他的鄰居，有特別的場合時他都會穿襯衫、打領帶，而且狄亞哥的身材和他差不多。狄亞哥很高興能幫得上這個忙，他還親自為布魯諾打領帶。這是布魯諾生平第一次打領帶。

「你怎麼會穿這種玩意？」布魯諾一邊問朋友，一邊拉著襯衫的領子，想把領帶弄鬆一點。

P.33

「你會習慣的，」他的朋友邊笑邊說道：「別再扯領子了，會弄亂的。」

布魯諾的媽媽這時走了進來，在那裡站了好一會兒，用充滿慈愛的眼神看著兒子。

「哎呀，你瞧瞧，我們這裡怎麼出現了這樣一位帥哥。」

「謝啦，媽。我好緊張，希望克蕾若的爸爸會喜歡我。」

「他怎麼可能會不喜歡你？你只要注意自己的舉止，不要裝模作樣就好了。就表現出你原來的樣子就可以，這才是克蕾若當初就是這樣喜歡上你的，不是嗎？」媽媽説完，又開心地咯咯笑著。

假裝

• 布魯諾的母親說「不要裝模作樣」，這句話是什麼意思？
• 你曾經故意裝模作樣過嗎？
• 你在面對不同的人時，你表現出的樣子都差不多嗎？

「現在該出發啦，好好玩吧。」母親一邊說，一邊給他一個擁吻。

布魯諾隨後連忙衝出門，生怕遲到。

P.34

還有五分鐘才八點，布魯諾來到了餐廳外面，這是他這輩子第一次來這種地方。他站在兩根大理石製的大廊柱之間，望著大門，看得目瞪口呆，臉上開始滑下豆大的汗珠。接著，他做了幾個深呼吸，他對自己説，走吧，該我們上啦。接著，他推開大門。

等他一踏進餐廳，他的那股自信瞬間消失。他第一次見識到這種地方：天花板上吊著大而眩目的水晶燈，地板上鋪著奢華厚重的絨毛地毯，每張圓桌上都鋪著白色的亞麻布桌巾，舒適的軟墊椅子上套著深紅色的緞質椅套。布魯諾看著每張桌子上琳瑯滿目的刀叉、湯匙、盤子和玻璃杯。

「噢，好傢伙，看來這種陣仗不好應付。」他心想。

這時，他看到克蕾若快步向他走過來，讓他鬆了一口氣。

「嗨，我沒有遲到吧？」他一邊問，

89

一邊在她臉頰上吻了一下。他怕她爸爸不會想看到他親吻她的嘴唇。

「你沒遲到，你來的正是時候，我們過去吧。我爸爸在那邊，等著見你。」

克蕾若拉著他的手，把他帶到爸爸的座位旁。佩卓起身相迎，禮貌地介紹了自己，然後很快地說道：「我已經為我們三個人訂了一桌美食，我想你喜歡吃 al dente 的通心粉。」

P. 36

「是的，當然。」布魯諾答道。不過他根本不知道 al dente 是什麼，只是菜都已經點好了，無所謂了。

席間的氣氛緊張兮兮的，整個現場的情況都讓布魯諾覺得很不自在。

讓人感到不自在的情況

・你碰到讓你感到不自在的情況嗎？跟夥伴分享。

・你當時是如何處理的？

一開始，佩卓還算和藹可親，但沒多久，客氣有禮的談話變成了一連串直接的問題，追問布魯諾的家庭和他對未來的計畫。

「你會給我女兒什麼樣的未來？」佩卓唐突地問道。

在布魯諾還沒來得及回答之前，有一對中年男女走到他們的桌子旁，扯起喉嚨喊道：「佩卓，想不到會在這裡碰到你！你最近還好嗎？」

佩卓立刻堆起笑容站起來，那是一位大客戶，偕同太座前來。這兩位不速之客，隨即在佩卓的桌邊坐了下來。佩卓簡單地把他們介紹給克蕾若和布魯諾認識。

P. 37

緊繃的氣氛一時之間緩和了下來，佩卓變得多話而友善。

佩卓的這位客戶卡洛斯向布魯諾笑了笑，問道：「布魯諾先生，請問你在哪兒高就？」

「我在工作。」布魯諾侷促不安地在椅子上挪動了一下位置回答道。

「是哪種工作？」

「販賣東西。」他繼續說道，不是很清楚應該怎麼說。

「他在一個販賣亭裡工作。」克蕾若突然插話補充道，好讓談話可以進行得順暢些。

「噢，原來你在開販賣亭，那很好啊，我想那可以輕輕鬆鬆賺到不少錢吧。」

「不是的，我是在海灘的一間販賣亭打工賣椰子汁。」布魯諾補充道。

四周頓時陷入一片安靜，氣氛變得很僵，僵到可以用刀把空氣切開。

後來，佩卓匆匆地買了單，大夥兒立刻鳥獸散。

從那晚之後，佩卓就認定布魯諾配不上他的人女兒。他很明白地對女兒說，布魯諾是個混血兒，和他們門不當、戶不對，他壓根反對他們兩個人交往。他要女兒不要再跟布魯諾見面，要她晚上待在家裡自己念書。

P.38

布魯諾和克蕾若

- 你覺得克蕾若的父親公平嗎？
- 你覺得父母親應該干涉子女的約會對象嗎？
- 你知道其他像布魯諾和克蕾若這樣被家長阻止見面的故事嗎？

P.39

不過，當然，克蕾若還是會趁著白天繼續和布魯諾偷偷約會。每天晚上，布魯諾在下班後回貧民區之前，都會來到她的公寓陽台下等著，好讓她給他一個飛吻，和他揮手道別。

克蕾若來到貧民區

P.40

克蕾若還沒去過布魯諾位在貧民區的家，她爸爸把她盯得很緊，尤其在那頓令人難忘的晚餐之後。布魯諾多次找她去他家玩，她也很想去認識他的家人，特別是他的母親。她很佩服布魯諾的母親，因為這位貧窮的單親媽媽獨力將三個子女拉拔長大。

後來，有這麼一天，佩卓突然說他週末要去聖保羅市出差，去參加一場家具展覽會。

他對克蕾若放不下心，克蕾若說她會找朋友來家裡一起溫習功課，也沒說她要去布魯諾家。

聽到克蕾若要來家裡，布魯諾很興奮。他趕緊通報媽媽，媽媽說她會煮她的拿手菜——黑豆燉肉。在貧民區裡，多娜・瑪麗亞的黑豆燉肉首屈一指，甚至，也有可能是全巴西最好吃的。

食物

• 黑豆燉肉是道典型的巴西美食，用黑豆、醃牛肉和豬肉燉煮而成。你的國家有什麼特色料理？你最喜歡吃的料理又是什麼？

P.41

到了星期六上午，布魯諾來克蕾若的公寓前接她，兩人先是搭公車來到貧民區的山腳下，然後再爬那些又長又陡、彎彎曲曲的階梯。

在來貧民區之前，克蕾若就做了番心理準備，但想不到這裡的人比她想像的還要貧窮。

他們一踏進布魯諾的屋子，多娜・瑪麗亞便立刻前來迎接，她把克蕾若攬入懷裡，親吻她的雙頰。

P.42

「克蕾若，歡迎你來我們家。能夠見到你，我太高興啦，布魯諾把你的事都跟我們說了。請把這裡當成你自己的家一樣，我們家雖然很簡陋，但決不會讓你餓到。我正在為你煮我最拿手的黑豆燉肉，馬上就可以開動了。」

「謝謝你，多娜・瑪麗亞，能夠來和你見面，真是太好了。」克蕾若說道。貧民區裡的這一切都讓她感到震驚，她還餘驚未息。

布魯諾接著帶她去客廳，她見到了布魯諾的弟弟和妹妹，還有平常一到星期六就會去他家一起享用午餐的一票親朋好友。只見每個人都伸開雙臂熱烈地歡迎克蕾若，氣氛顯得輕鬆又友善，彷彿一下子大家生下來就互相認識了一樣。

吃過午餐後，他們移師到平坦開闊的屋頂，這時樂器不知道從哪裡冒了出來，一下子的功夫，大家不是開始玩起樂器，就是隨著森巴舞的節拍開始唱唱跳跳起來。只見各式各樣的鼓一應俱全，還有弦樂器、鈴鼓、搖鈴、刮片、鈴等。布魯諾挑了一只魁卡鼓，那是會發出高聲調、短促尖聲的一種鼓。克蕾若跟著旋律用腳打拍子，笑得很開懷。

「我覺得自己好笨，什麼樂器都不會。」她湊到布魯諾的耳邊說道，覺得自己打不進他們的圈子裡。

P. 44

「玩樂器，你當然會啦，這個給你。」布魯諾邊笑邊說道。他遞了一個口哨給她，「你什麼時候想吹就吹，決不會出錯的。」

大夥兒就這樣玩樂器、又唱又跳了一整個下午，一直玩到向晚時分。克蕾若已經記不起來，自己有多久沒有這樣盡興地玩了。

音樂

- 你喜歡聽哪一類的音樂？你喜歡的歌星或樂團有哪些？
- 你會彈奏樂器嗎？是什麼樂器？
- 你希望自己會玩樂器嗎？你想玩什麼樣的樂器？

克蕾若以前常聽別人講貧民區的瘋克舞派對，但她沒有親眼見過。現在她好不容易有機會去見識，便央求布魯諾晚上帶她去開一下眼界。她在家裡是聽過這類的音樂：放克節奏，配上鮮明的饒舌風格歌詞，歌詞大多觸及重要的社會議題，像是貧窮、種族主義、暴力或是正義等等。

P. 45

他們朝舞廳走去，克蕾若一方面感到興奮，一方面也有點緊張，不是很放得開。她爸爸要是發現她跑到這種地方來，一定會抓狂的。

饒舌樂

- 饒舌樂這個字是由數個單字的字首所組成的，RAP 這三個字母分別代表哪些字？
- 你喜歡饒舌樂嗎？你知道有哪些知名的饒舌歌手嗎？
- 你覺得音樂能夠改變社會嗎？會如何改變？和夥伴想想看，有哪些歌曲對人們的思想和行為造成了很大的影響？

當他們來到舞廳時，偌大的舞廳早已塞爆，裡面擠滿了有幾百個貧民區的年輕人。裡頭的音樂震耳欲聾，每個角落裡的人都像瘋了一樣地跳著舞。克蕾若覺得格格不入，而布魯諾始終都用臂膀緊緊環抱住她，讓她感到溫暖而安全。

P. 46

沒一會兒，她轉向布魯諾，說道：「我們可以走了嗎？我覺得不太舒服，這地方不太適合我，你不會生氣吧？」

「當然不會。」布魯諾笑著說：「這裡也不合我的口味，我想你也不會喜歡。我先去上個廁所，你待在這裡不要離開，我馬上就回來，好嗎？」

克蕾若看著布魯諾鑽進人群裡，很快便消失不見。不一會兒，一個高大魁梧的男人出現在她的面前。那個人穿著一件白色的緊身T恤，炫耀雙臂的肌肉。

克蕾若見狀連忙閃開，心想：「這個彪形大漢要對我幹嘛？」

但男人跟了上來，靠她很近，她感覺到他味道很重的呼吸熱氣，正襲向自己的臉上。

「嗨，寶貝，你這樣一個漂亮的富家千金，怎麼會來這種地方？」

克蕾若一陣驚慌，她一顆心砰砰地跳著，只求布魯諾趕快回來。

恐懼
- 克蕾若很害怕，想像如果你處在她的情況下，你會怎麼做？
- 回想一下曾經讓你害怕的經驗，當時發生了什麼事？你又如何處理？
- 把你害怕的事情列出來，和夥伴分享。

P. 47

「我和我男朋友一起來，他去上個廁所，很快就會回來。」克蕾若力做鎮定，雖然她其實很想哭。

男子這時用臂膀勾住克蕾若的肩膀，臉上露出輕浮的獰笑，糾纏道：「別這樣，趁等他的空檔，我們來跳支舞。」

但就在這個時候，布魯諾向他衝過來。

「札加，把你的手放開！」布魯諾大聲喝斥道。

之後，布魯諾突然感到腦袋的兩邊一陣劇痛，是札加這位彪形大漢的兩個保鑣，他們用槍猛擊布魯諾的雙耳。布魯諾僵在那兒，整個人嚇呆了。

「行啦。」那傢伙吼道，一邊大聲地笑著，「讓他走，他是我的朋友，對吧，布魯諾？嗨，老兄，好久不見了，是吧？最近可好？真沒想到，你還帶著一個這麼正的馬子！」

「一切都好，老兄。」布魯諾回答道。

在一陣讓人神經緊繃的安靜之後，布魯諾接著說：「現在我們得走了，好嗎？那麼，回頭見了，是吧？」

P. 48

「是啊，回頭見了，老兄。保重了。」札加點點頭，帶著恐嚇的神情說道。

布魯諾做了個深呼吸，然後給克蕾若一個滿懷歉意的微笑。克蕾若還在打哆嗦，布魯諾牽起她的手，靜靜地緩步離開，不敢回頭看。

布魯諾有一股不祥的預感，他知道他很快就會再見到札加。

一肚子壞水的札加

P.49

札加是荷西‧卡洛斯‧桑多仕的乳名，他長大後，大家還是都叫他札加。札加的塊頭一直都比同年齡的孩子高大魁梧，所以常會欺負比他瘦小的人。沒多久，附近的小孩子都怕他，他說的話沒有人敢不聽。

欺負

- 你小時候被欺負過嗎？你認識什麼喜歡欺負人的人嗎？
- 和夥伴想想看，有什麼方法可以制止這種恃強凌弱的行為。

長大後的札加，是這一帶身材最高大的人。為了讓自己更強壯，札加每天下午都會把時間花在當地的一家健身房裡練舉重。一個肌肉結實的彪形大漢，沒有人惹得起。

P.50

札加很小便學會如何照顧自己。在他八歲的時候，他父親就因為偷車去坐牢，而他的母親也很少在家，所以他必須自己想辦法活下去。

很快地，他開始偷小東西，又過沒多久，他就開始了重大的罪行，像是行搶和勒索。他很慓悍，才十八歲的年紀，就成了一票罪犯和流氓的頭頭。

其實早在札加十三歲時，他就開始了第一次的拉幫結派，把貧民區的毛賊召集起來。貧民區的男孩會在當地的一小

片空地上踢足球，札加和他的手下當時就控制了比賽。

P.51

那時布魯諾才十歲，他常去看大孩子們踢足球，每個孩子都夢想變成像艾杜安奴那樣的足球明星，永遠地離開貧民區。

這一天，札加的球隊少了一名隊員，當時他仔細地掃視了一下球場四周牆上坐著的年輕觀眾，他們等在那裡看開賽。結果札加相中了布魯諾，他大喊道：「小子，想下來玩玩嗎？」

「我嗎？」布魯諾驚訝地問道，吃驚得無法相信自己的耳朵。

「不然你以為我在跟誰說話？」札加吼道，開始有點惱火了。

P.52

布魯諾立刻興奮地從牆上一躍而下，跑進足球場。

這是一場硬仗，上半場結束時，札加的球隊還以一比零落後。布魯諾上半場是打後衛的位置，不過就在下半場要開始之前，札加把布魯諾叫過來說：「我要把你換到前鋒的位置，你要好好表現！」接著他又語帶要脅地說：「你最少要射進兩分，我的球隊是沒輸過的，懂嗎？」

布魯諾很害怕，不過當比賽再度開始後，他就忘了札加的話，只想著要贏球。他表現得很出色，踢進了漂亮的兩球，他隊上的另外一名男孩也射進一球，比賽結果是三比一，他們贏了！

「不賴嘛，老兄。」比賽結束後札加對他說：「你隨時都可以來和我們一起玩，知道嗎？」

「謝啦，札加。」布魯諾雖然這樣

回答，但他心裡頭知道這並不是什麼好事。

在贏了那場足球比賽之後，布魯諾在貧民區裡也得到了札加的保護，沒有人敢找他的麻煩。布魯諾對這一點感激在心，可是札加還想要拉他進入犯罪幫派，而這是布魯諾所深惡痛絕的。

在那場比賽之後的幾年間，因為要討好札加，布魯諾偶而會下場比賽。不過自從他開始在販賣亭賣椰子汁之後，已經有兩年沒下場踢球，或是看到札加了。

P.53

直到現在，他們才再度重逢，不過在舞池上和札加的巧遇，讓布魯諾很憂心，他知道札加遲早會找上門的。

而札加的出現，比布魯諾預期的還快。在舞池巧遇後一個星期左右，就在布魯諾下班回家時，狹窄的暗巷裡突然走出來兩個男人，把他推到牆邊。兩人用手臂一把抓住他，其中一個人說道：「札加現在想見見你，跟我們走。」

他們把他拖過幾條街道，然後推他走下幾個台階，進入旁邊的一個房子裡。札加已經在那裡候駕了，他坐在一張高腳凳上，自顧自地吹著口哨。

「嗨，布魯諾，真高興看到你來看老朋友啦。」他皮笑肉不笑地說：「坐下，我有正經事要跟你說。」

札加跟他講了一個萬無一失的計畫，他要去偷大學聯考的考卷，然後在考試的前一天兜售。他認識印考卷的印刷公司裡的一個人，對方會挾帶一份考卷出來給他。

P.54

「現在有個用得著你的地方，」他繼續解釋道：「你和你那位有錢的漂亮馬子，可以幫我把考卷賣給伊帕尼瑪區的有錢人家子弟。當然，我也會把考卷給你和你馬子，這樣你們兩個人就都可以上大學啦，這不就是你一直想要的嗎？是不是，布魯諾？」

布魯諾

- 你認為布魯諾會怎麼做？
- 如果是你的話，你會怎麼做？
- 你會給布魯諾什麼樣的建議？

布魯諾一言不發地坐了下來，他很震驚。還沒等到他鎮定下來，札加繼續說道：「噢，還有，你要是敢玩花樣，擺我們的道，克蕾若和她爸爸住在什麼地方，我們是很清楚的，我們隨時都可以去拜訪他們，給他們驚喜，但我想他們不會樂意見到我們吧。」

札加說完之後，一陣狂笑聲。面色慘白的布魯諾則被帶到外面。

布魯諾陷入兩難

P.55

布魯諾著實進退兩難。

一方面，他現在可以很快擺脫貧民區這種沒有未來的生活，如果幫札加賣偷來的考卷，那他就一定能上一流大學，這是一張穩妥的通行證，可以讓他有一個更好的未來，這是通往財富、甚至是幸福的捷徑。

不過另一方面，札加要他做非法的勾當，但他認為，社會需要規範和制度，違反規範、破壞制度是錯誤的行為，在道德上是說不過去的。

布魯諾的媽媽始終在教導他認識是非對錯，要他知道遵守法律是很重要的。

但布魯諾又想，如果不照札加的話去做，克蕾若和她父親的性命就會受到嚴重的威脅。

布魯諾不知道該如何抉擇，他在正當做事和迅速擺脫貧困生活之間搖擺。

P.56

對與錯

- 如果你面臨到布魯諾的處境，你會怎麼做？
- 原本不正當的事，有可能變成正當的嗎？如果有可能，那是什麼樣的情況？

布魯諾絞盡腦汁想要擺脫這個困境，最後他做出了決定。

他還沒有把他和札加碰面的事告訴克蕾若，他知道克蕾若一定會嚇壞的。但他現在應該把一切事情都跟她講了，並且説出自己的決定。他們在克蕾若家的公寓大廈前面碰頭，布魯諾慢慢地把所有事情都告訴她。之後，他打電話給札加。

「好，札加，我們照你的話做。不過你要先答應我，克蕾若和她爸爸絕對不會受到傷害。」

「那還有什麼問題，我說到做到。差不多要行動了，布魯諾，你馬上到我這裡來，幫裡的其他弟兄也都會到，我們會跟你講全部的細節。」

接著札加指示布魯諾，要他先到貧民區一個街角那邊的倉庫，和札加的一位手下會合，然後再帶他去幫派的巢穴。

P.57

果然，一個滿臉邪氣的高個子已經在那裡等候了。他帶著布魯諾沿著狹窄又曲折的小徑往上走，最後來到山頂上一處最高的地方。

當時正值日正當中，灼灼陽光直射而下，讓布魯諾覺得一路上都被人監視著。他摘下太陽眼鏡，拿著手帕擦眉頭。當札加和他的手下出現在視線裡時，他才把眼鏡戴上，把手帕塞回口袋裡。那票人當時正圍坐在屋子後院的一張大桌子上玩牌。

「嗨，布魯諾，真高興看到你，老兄。過來這裡，見見這幫好兄弟。」札加高聲喊道。

在布魯諾還沒來得及行動時，就有兩個守哨的來搜他的身了。那兩個家伙搜查他的身體，查看是否藏有槍刀什麼武器時，布魯諾露出了畏縮的神情。

「他很乾淨，老大。」其中一人大聲叫道。

札加一一跟他介紹了幫派的成員，包括在印刷廠工作、準備偷考卷的男子。接著，札加説明計畫的所有細節。這個計畫看起來萬無一失，不可能會出差錯。

大家互相握了握手，然後閃人。

布魯諾的心臟砰砰地跳個飛快，他只想趕快遠離這幫人，然後打電話給克蕾若。

P.58

他飛奔下山，到了山腳下才停下腳步。他回過頭，後面沒有人，沒有人在跟蹤他，他這才掏出電話，打給克蕾若。

「嗨，克蕾若，現在事情都在按計畫進行中，」他上氣不接下氣地説：「當然，是按我的計畫，不是按札加的計畫。」他補充道，興奮地笑著。

廢棄工廠

P.59

「太妙了！」在警局裡，警官看著端坐在前面的布魯諾和克蕾若，不禁咧開嘴笑了，「你們做得很好，你們是怎樣想出這麼妙的計畫的？」

「謝啦，我想得要夠機靈才行。」布魯諾回答道，他禮貌地笑了笑，感謝警官的稱讚。「你相信嗎，我是在洗澡的時候突然想出來的。我記得我在網路上看過一個可偷拍的特殊太陽眼鏡的廣告，眼鏡裡頭內藏了小型的攝影機，這種東西本來只提供給偵探和執法機關使用，不過在網路上誰都可以買得到。」

布魯諾在和札加那幫人碰面之前，已經先和克蕾若談過了，他們兩個人都認為，偷考卷、幫札加賣考卷給別人，是錯誤的行為。布魯諾最後想出了一個很妙的計畫，不但可以騙過札加，也可以讓自己不被捲進去。

P.60

首先，他假裝同意札加的計畫，去和那票盜賊碰面。當他去到他們的巢穴時，他們雖然對他搜過身，查看有無藏匿武器，卻沒有想到布魯諾戴的太陽眼鏡藏了小型的攝影機。

布魯諾把整個會面過程都偷偷地錄了影，並刻意對每個幫派成員都做了近距離攝影。過程中的談話，連同計畫的所有細節，也都錄音下來了

接下來，等他一確定自己沒被跟蹤時，就打電話給克蕾若，然後帶著攝影

機和她一起上警察局，跟警方說明整個情況。

「謝謝你提供這些證據，我們終於可以抓到札加那幫作案的歹徒了。」警官繼續說道：「可是，我們還需要你和克蕾若的協助，很重要的是，你們兩個要裝作沒事地繼續配合下去。札加要你們做什麼，你們就一定要配合他。從現在開始，我們會跟蹤你們的每一步行動，你們凡事都照札加所說的去做就行，可以嗎？」

接著警方又去那家印刷廠，把事情的原委告訴了老闆。對方同意和警方合作，也讓警方在那裡安置了一些隱藏式攝影機。

到了偷考卷的那一天，他們目睹到那名內賊用監視攝影機把試卷照下來，不過警方仍按兵不動，他們要等到札加展開下一步的行動。

P.61

兩天之後，布魯諾一如往常在販賣亭裡工作時，他的電話響了，是札加打來的。札加要他和克蕾若一起到城外數英哩遠的一家廢棄舊工廠，考卷已經準備好了。

布魯諾於是打電話給克蕾若，叫她盡快到販賣亭跟他碰面，一起去廢棄工廠。接著，他再打電話給警方，跟警方說明細節。

當布魯諾和克蕾若到達時，所有的幫派成員已經在那裡等他們。只見大伙兒笑鬧著，慶祝他們成功地偷到考卷。

布魯諾和克蕾若也加入他們的行列，並且開始打開背包，向偷來的考卷瞄了一眼。

這時，大門突然被猛地撞開，傳來語氣很堅定的大聲說話聲：「我們是警察！把你們的槍放下！跪下，把雙手放在頭上！」

不過接下來是一陣槍響聲，聽不到警方接著又說了什麼。現場的人四處奔竄，骯髒的舊地板上塵土飛揚。

這時忽然傳出一陣粗嘎的聲音，大喊了幾次：「停火！」

P.63

這時大家都安靜了下來，飛揚的塵土開始慢慢落下，只見札加站在屋子的中間，拿著槍抵住克蕾若的頭，他狂叫道：「把槍扔掉，然後踢到這裡來，再趴到地板上，每個人都得照做，不然她就沒命！」

警察於是紛紛扔下了佩槍，並朝著札加那裡踢去。這時，有一把槍在地上彈了起來，飛落在布魯諾的正前方，當時布魯諾正跪在札加後方的地板上。

布魯諾不假思索，幾乎是本能地抓起槍，朝著札加的腳扣了扳機。札加應聲倒地，克蕾若立刻跑向布魯諾。

這時有更多武裝警察衝了進來，很快控制了現場，札加和其他的幫派成員很快被扣上手銬，帶往在外等候的警車。

克蕾若鑽進布魯諾的臂膀裡，不住地哭泣和顫抖。兩人一語不發，驚魂未定。

勇氣

· 回想你曾經展現出勇氣的時刻，跟夥伴分享當時發生了什麼事，你又做了什麼事。

落幕

P.64

（一個月之後）

在警方那次奇襲結束後不久，布魯諾和克蕾若參加了大學的入學考試，結果雙雙通過測驗，進入了一流的學府。

有關當局很感謝布魯諾和克蕾若阻止盜售考卷的事情發生，因此他們不但拿到了全額獎學金，還榮獲政府所頒發的高額補助金，以應付他們四年求學期間的一切生活開支。

在一個星期六，克蕾若的爸爸佩卓在自家公寓裡舉辦了慶祝的午餐會。布魯諾此時一個人站在陽台上，凝視著外面的大海，這時佩卓走了過來，站在他旁邊。

佩卓有些生硬地對布魯諾笑了笑，說道：「布魯諾，我真心誠意想跟你道歉。我第一次看到你的時候，認為你配不上我的女兒，不過現在，很確定的是，我很高興你有勇氣做你自己。還有，你救了她一命！你的大恩大德，難以回報。請原諒我。」佩卓看著布魯諾，眼中閃著淚光。

P.66

原諒

- 如果你是布魯諾，你會原諒佩卓嗎？
- 回想你曾經原諒過別人的經驗，以及別人原諒過你的經驗。

「我當然會原諒你，」布魯諾露出溫暖的笑容，「這段時間大家都不好過，不過總算都圓滿落幕了，不是嗎？」

他們給了彼此一個擁抱，什麼話都沒說。之後，布魯諾才打破沉默。

「不知道午餐是不是準備好了，我好餓啊！」他說。

接著，廚房裡傳來一陣聲調抑揚頓挫的愉快叫喊聲。

「大家要準備開動囉。」只見多娜·瑪麗亞得意洋洋地宣布。

「你知道嗎，布魯諾。」佩卓大聲地說道：「al dente 通心粉，永遠也打不過你媽媽的黑豆燉肉！」

他們一邊衝進餐廳，一邊開懷地大笑起來。

Before Reading

Page 6

1

a) 2   b) 3   c) 1   d) 3   e) 1
f) 2   g) 1   h) 2   i) 3   j) 1

Page 8

4

- **Bruno**: optimistic, enthusiastic, hard-working, poor, shy
- **Clara**: bad-tempered, gorgeous, anxious, rich, fair-skinned
- **Zeca**: tough, menacing, muscular, criminal, thug

5

- The coconut seller is Bruno. The hero in the story is Bruno; the villain is Zeca.
- Bruno is the hero because he looks optimistic, enthusiastic and hard-working. Zeca is the villain because he looks tough, menacing and cruel.

Page 9

6

a) adventure / drama
b) a robbery; dreams comes true

8

a) 10   b) 1   c) 2   d) 7   e) 8   f) 11
g) 5   h) 3   i) 4   j) 12   k) 6   l) 9

Page 11

10

2. Bruno
3. Bruno meets Clara
1. Bruno meets Clara's father
4. The abandoned factory

Page 30

- **PARENTS**

Clara has a bad relationship with her father; he wants to control her life and she fights against this attitude.

Page 33

- **PRETENDING**

Bruno's mum means that he must present himself as he is. He must not make other people believe that he is a different person.

Page 45

- **RAP**

Rap stands for Rhythm And Poetry.

After Reading

Page 68

10

a) F b) T c) D d) T e) T f) F
g) T h) D i) F j) T k) F l) D

11

a) Because he wanted to change his life, to seize the opportunity to make his life extraordinary.
b) Because she was able to go to the favela to visit Bruno's family.
c) Because he wanted to catch Zeca and his gang red-handed. He really planned to tell the police.

Page 69

15

a) 5 b) 4 c) 10 d) 2 e) 1
f) 8 g) 9 h) 3 i) 7 j) 6

Page 70

17

a) Clara to Bruno, when she sees him at the kiosk reading a Portuguese novel.
b) Bruno to Zeca, when Zeca asks Clara to dance with him at the baile funk dance party.
c) Dona Maria to Bruno, when Bruno was very young and wanted to know why they couldn't live in the rich apartments.

d) Clara to Bruno, after the lunch at Bruno's house, when they are all playing musical instruments.
e) Zeca to Bruno, when he asked Bruno to play in his football team a few years ago.
f) Bruno to Clara, the afternoon after they met, when Clara realizes he is serious about studying literature.
g) Pedro to Bruno, at the end of the story when Pedro organizes a celebration lunch in his apartment.
h) Zeca to Clara, when he tries to dance with her at the *baile funk* dance party.
i) Pedro to Clara, when the concierge tells him of a young man dating his daughter.
j) Bruno to Clara, after secretly recording the gang meeting.

Page 71

18

• **Bruno**: dark brown eyes, jet-black hair, good-looking, slim, cheerful
• **Clara**: beautiful, fair-skinned, blonde hair, young, gorgeous
• **Zeca**: heavy-set, big, muscular, tall, smelly breath
• **Pedro**: well-dressed, distinguished-looking, tall, in his late forties, hair turning gray at the sides

105

Page 72

21

a) 8   b) 3   c) 4   d) 10   e) 1
f) 13   g) 7   h) 5   i) 2   j) 12
k) 6   l) 9   m) 11

Page 73

23

Places mentioned in the story: Rio de Janeiro, Ipanema beach, a favela called Morro do Cantagalo, a kiosk on the beach, Clara's apartment, an elegant Italian restaurant, Dona Maria's house, the roof of the house, a dance hall, the football playing field in the favela, a house where Bruno meets Zeca, a store on one of the street corners in the favela (i.e. the gang's hideout), the police station, the abandoned factory,

26

Bruno saw a movie called *Dead Poets Society*, which profoundly impressed him. Sometimes later he got his first job selling coconuts and coconut water at a small kiosk in Ipanema. Then one day Bruno met Clara when she went to the kiosk to buy coconut water. They started studying together and after a very short time they started dating. Soon after, Bruno went to the Italian restaurant to meet Clara's father. Later Clara went to the favela to meet Bruno's family and Bruno took her to a *baile funk* dance party in the favela. But Zeca annoyed Clara when she was on her own at the party. The following week, Zeca's bodyguards took Bruno to see him and Zeca "invited" Bruno to take part in his plan to steal and sell exams. Sometime later Bruno went to the police with recorded evidence of the plan and Zeca and his gang were arrested. One month later, Bruno and Clara passed the university entrance exams and also got a full scholarship and a grant.

Page 74

28

a) 7   b) 5   c) 10   d) 3   e) 1
f) 6   g) 9   h) 4   i) 8   j) 2

Page 75

29

a) 1   b) 3   c) 3   d) 2

30

a) 8   b) 5   c) 9   d) 10   e) 2   f) 1
g) 11   h) 3   i) 6   j) 4   k) 12   l) 7

Test

Page 76

1
a) F   b) F   c) T   d) T   e) F
f) T   g) F   h) F   i) T   j) F
k) T   l) T   m) F   n) T   o) F

2

a) Bruno lived in a favela.
b) "Carpe Diem" was a quote from his favorite movie.
e) Bruno wanted to study Portuguese Language and Literature.
g) Pedro was angry when he found that Clara was dating Bruno.
h) Bruno arrived on time.
j) Clara felt it was not her scene.
m) They were not killed. They were arrested.
o) Clara's dad, Pedro, organized a celebration lunch at his apartment.

Page 77
3
a) 1   b) 3   c) 2   d) 1   e) 3
f) 1   g) 3   h) 1   i) 3   j) 2

國家圖書館出版品預行編目資料

里約小情歌 / Jack Scholes 著；李璞良 譯. —初
版. —[臺北市]：寂天文化, 2012.10　面；公分.

中英對照

ISBN 978-986-318-043-2 (25K平裝附光碟片)

1.英語 2.讀本

805.18　　　　　　　　　101019450

作者 _ Jack Scholes
譯者 _ 李璞良
校對 _ 陳慧莉
封面設計 _ 蔡怡柔
主編 _ 黃鈺云
製程管理 _ 蔡智堯
出版者 _ 寂天文化事業股份有限公司
電話 _ +886-2-2365-9739
傳真 _ +886-2-2365-9835
網址 _ www.icosmos.com.tw
讀者服務 _ onlineservice@icosmos.com.tw
出版日期 _ 2012年10月 初版一刷（250101）
郵撥帳號 _ 1998620-0 寂天文化事業股份有限公司
訂購金額600 （含）元以上郵資免費
訂購金額600元以下者，請外加郵資60元
若有破損，請寄回更換

〔限台灣銷售〕